I0525501

THE LUST LIST: DEVON STONE

# SECOND CHANCES

## MIRA BAILEE

NoMi Press

Copyright © 2014 by Mira Bailee
Cover design by Qamber Designs
Editing by Nicole Bailey, Proof Before You Publish

All rights reserved. No part of this publication may be reproduced, distributed, or transmitted in any form or by any means, including photocopying, recording, or other electronic or mechanical methods, without the prior written permission of the publisher, except in the case of brief quotations embodied in critical reviews and certain other noncommercial uses permitted by copyright law.

Euphoria Publishing
NoMi Press
www.euphoriapublishing.com

Publisher's Note: This is a work of fiction. Names, characters, places, and incidents are a product of the author's imagination, and any resemblance to actual people, living or dead, or to businesses, companies, events, institutions, or locales is completely coincidental.

ISBN-13: 978-0692348734
ISBN-10: 0692348735

Printed in the United States of America

*For everyone who has taken a leap
to give the one they love another chance.*

# CHAPTER ONE

Ten minutes ago, I was Olivia Margot–a mediocre, distracted assistant to an asshole event coordinator. But a few shots, some temporary confidence, and the unwavering encouragement only my best friend Maddie can give, and now I'm Superstar O, the one sitting in the backseat of Devon's Benz, taking control.

"Well?" I ask as I stare into Devon's bright blue eyes. He looks as surprised as I feel.

Devon leaps into the car after me, his millionaire grin a mile wide. "You're serious?"

Of course I'm serious. This entire past week has been a whirlwind. Devon got me the very job I just walked out on. He spent the few days I've now known him being equally mysterious and frustrating. And through all the chaos of trying to work for an impossible-to-satisfy Mr. Keenly, Devon was the one highlight—even with his drama. He's the one who protected me from the paparazzi. He's the one who went out of his way to make me smile. And he's the one who just picked me over his gorgeous, rock star ex-girlfriend, Kennedy Rose.

Is it really that earth-shattering that I can make impulsive decisions and act in favor of my own well-being? Yes, I suppose it is. But I was tired of Keenly being a jerk and getting away with it. And I was infuriated with Kennedy and her sense of entitlement when it came to who got Devon. You know what, bitch? *I* got Devon.

I rest my dizzy head against the back of the seat, my entire body tipsy and light as if it's been lifted up on a cloud. I push out the irritated voice in my mind reminding me how irresponsible I'm being–how I told off Keenly, quit my job, and just left all my things back with Maddie in order to run off on an impromptu excursion with Devon. It's only for the night. I don't need my purse, my phone. I need the man sitting beside me.

"Do I look like I'm bluffing?" I say to him. Why would I jump into the car first if I'd intended to bail? "Now let's get moving before my buzz wears off."

He pulls the door shut as Mark shifts into drive and circles the driveway, looping back toward our exit. I look behind us one last time. The gorgeous mansion, all lit up and bustling inside and out. The front door opens as a woman in a green dress rushes out, looking upset. There's too much drama in this Hollywood world, but I've made my choice. I'm a part of it now. If it means getting to be with Devon, then I'll take it all. Past the crying girl, through the double doors, I see the party in full motion. There was no sudden implosion when I told my boss to fuck off.

The house didn't crumble just because I left early. And not a soul inside knew I was currently ditching all of them to make my getaway with *The* Devon Stone...Well, except for Kennedy.

And that thought couldn't please me more.

No, the world didn't stop spinning because I'd made a spontaneous decision. In fact, the only lives affected were Devon's and my own, and it could only get better from here.

Devon leans in and kisses me. "So you have to be drunk to be into me? You taste like cinnamon and something fruity."

That would be courtesy of bartender Maddie who likes to surprise me with each drink. I focus on my words to be sure I'm not slurring. "Let's call it," I articulate each syllable, "personality reinforcement." I giggle and my veins pump with adrenaline. "And I don't need it to know I'm very much *into you.*"

"Elaborate, Miss Margot." Devon's voice is commanding. "Tell me what you're into."

I smile, soaking in these moments when I can flirt with him candidly. "I'm into your messy hair," I say, raking my fingers through his dark locks. "And your sexy scowl. And the way you don't put up with anything. It's like everything about you is filled with excitement."

Devon's eyes are on me. On my purple designer gown, on my carefully styled hair, on my smooth legs that feel hollow from drunkenness. Thankfully, we're sitting. I wish I knew what he was thinking, but all I can do is stare at his sly grin as his gaze moves away from me and out the window. Where is he taking me, anyway?

"So you tell me. What are you into about me?" Er...what about me are–or why are you–never mind. He gets my point. Damn alcohol makes me speak like a fool.

But he doesn't answer. Instead, he puts a hand on my thigh, and I bask in the tingling warmth that washes over me while I try to keep myself from saying anything else that could sound stupid. But *why* is he into me? There's no doubt that I'm different from the others, but I can't tell why it's a good thing. I lack the celebrity experience and social status and...bank account that he must be accustomed to with other women he's dated. I'll only be a challenge, but there's no denying what I can feel growing between us. How every interaction and every time he's near me, I feel like...like I could fly. I feel more alive and more like the person I want to be when Devon is with me. How do I make him feel?

He stretches out his legs, and I laugh at his carefree ensemble of the night. He's ditched his suit jacket, leaving him with the designer jeans and vintage t-shirt.

"You went all out tonight," I quip. "Wasn't this a black tie affair?" I run my fingers along his side, and he grabs my hand, holding it tight and pulling me closer to him.

"You don't think I look good?" he says in my ear, his voice low.

He looks damn good, and I'm certain he knows it. I move in and kiss him, my tongue enticing him to bring me closer. His mouth tastes like liquor–we both needed that liquid courage tonight. Standing up to my boss was nothing compared to how Devon had to get up in front of everyone and congratulate his family for screwing him over. What will he do now? And how do I fit into it?

His strong arms wrap around me, hugging me close. Here, I'm safe. I'm secure. I don't care that I don't know what will happen to-morrow. Or that I'm disconnected from the rest of the world. The scent of Devon's cologne and the heat from his body embrace me as I pull away from his lips and settle against his chest. This is exactly where I want to be.

Devon's hand leisurely runs along my side and down my thigh. The light touch from his fingertips sends electric shocks through me, and I press myself into him even closer.

We're far from the Stone residence and heading away from the coast. My head still spins from bravery and alcohol, and I feel like we're rising higher and higher on our own private Ferris wheel. I'm inching closer to the moon with my dream man by my side, when I feel the Benz come to a stop.

I sit up, looking out the windows. "Where are we?"

Parked in an empty parking garage, all I see are the black windows of a dark, empty building.

"You want excitement, right?" Devon asks as he opens the door and climbs out.

"Well, yeah–um." I stumble out behind him, regaining my balance by grabbing ahold of Devon's elbow.

I turn back around to grab my purse. Oh right, I abandoned it at the Stone mansion. Suddenly I feel naked without my trusty cell phone. But I'm with Devon. And he wants me to give him another chance. To trust him. So without any other option, I guess I will.

Devon seems so nonchalant as we walk toward the dark building in front of us.

"This place looks closed." Of course it is. It's the middle of the night, and it looks like a regular old office building. Where has he taken me?

He ignores me and approaches the doors. A discreet metal panel hangs on a wall near the left door. Devon slides it open to reveal a keypad. He punches in a code, and the doors make a clicking sound. My mind floods with questions. Dozens of "what's" and "how's". But that's every situation with Devon. He's got mischief up his sleeve.

He pulls open the, now, unlocked door and holds his arm out to invite me in. It's pitch-black in there, and I can't help but wonder if we're trespassing.

"Devon, I don't know. I don't think we should be here." Is he trying to get us both arrested?

Since I hesitated, he walks in ahead of me, and I have to quickly catch the door before it closes. I'm either stranded in the scary, empty parking garage, or I'm breaking and entering into a business. Am I really expected to choose here?

*Trust him.* But why? He's already proven he's sneaky, and the tabloids have put him in the spotlight every time he's broken the law. So how can I explain the closeness I still feel to him, knowing that he's unpredictable? Reckless? The last thing I should do, if we're speaking logically, is trust him. But my decreasing inhibition takes over, and I feel the unexplainable magnetic pull that I have toward him. I want him. I'll go anywhere with him.

I follow Devon inside, and dim motion-sensor lights brighten the room enough to see rows of cubicles. What exactly is he planning on finding here? Or stealing?

He leads me beyond the cubicles toward another set of closed doors. It's as if we're making our way to the corporate offices. Like we're about to commit some sort of heist.

"Can you tell me where we're going, or should I sort out my alibi now?"

He turns back, only to give me a mischievous grin as he pulls out a set of keys and unlocks these doors.

"I'm serious, Devon. What is this? I didn't go with you to–"

He opens the door to reveal a much brighter hallway. Shielding my eyes, I'm ready to flee. My throat constricts and my heart palpitates. This is too weird. But Devon strolls right in like this is perfectly normal.

"If we get caught–if we get in trouble–" I say.

He raises a hand to quiet me. I'm starting to think he's having fun leading me on.

"No. Don't tell me not to talk. Whatever you're doing. I don't want to anymore. Let's go back. Is Mark still with the Benz?" Damn. If I had my purse... My pulse is racing, and my legs are growing heavier. They don't want to move a step closer. My whole body is objecting to whatever Devon's brought us into. "I'll go back out. Mark can take me back to the house. You can stay and–"

"Good evening, Mr. Stone."

I shriek and almost jump out of my skin. We've been caught. I knew it. Apparently, he wasn't expecting the large-windowed office halfway down this hall. A man in a black suit sits behind a computer, but...he knew Devon's name.

"Evening, Carl." Devon nods at the man as we continue past him. So it's okay that we're here?

Another set of doors waits at the end of this hall, and I can only imagine what will be on the other side. A science lab? A bookstore? A three-ring circus?

But we stop short at an elevator instead. I'm just going with it. My curiosity has woken up, and this ridiculous game of follow the leader has to end sometime.

Devon punches in another code, and the doors slide open for us.

I sigh and follow him in as he pulls out a card and scans it, then presses a button with a 'P' on it. *Going up.*

"Alright. Tell me," I say. "This is getting—"

He shuts me up by slamming his lips into mine, pressing me into the cold wall of the elevator. My nerves are already a wreck, and now they ignite with my lust for Devon. My heart beats an unsteady rhythm—quickening as we rise higher and higher. From one floor to the next to the next, he kisses me until I hear a beep and we stop. The doors open, and I'm astonished by what I see.

"Is this your...?" Words fail me as I take in the vast space. Dark wood floors and rustic, industrial furnishings... It's oversized, yet the perfect fit for a wealthy bachelor.

"My condo, yeah."

We walk into the open space and toward the living room area. I take in the copper light fixtures, leather couches, and a steel entertainment center that holds a massive flat screen and other electronics. I'm impressed by the classiness of it, though it's still clearly a bachelor pad. An empty beer bottle sits on a side table and video game controllers lay on the couch.

I turn a full one-eighty to find the kitchen at the other end. An enormous island in the middle matches the same industrial feel as the living room–brushed metal and solid wood. Aside from a few dirty dishes piled in the sink, the kitchen is big enough and nice enough to suit a top chef.

Between us and the kitchen, an iron staircase twists up to an upstairs loft. Not that I'm in a hurry to see Devon's bed, but...

I turn back toward Devon again, and he's sporting his grin.

"You know you had me freaked out wandering around this strange place," I say.

"I know."

"So does it always take a private staff and multiple detours to get you home?"

He kicks his shoes off, and slides them toward a wall. One stops by a table while the other rolls into the entryway. *Such a guy*.

"That's nothing," he says. "My other condo requires a helicopter drop-off and six guard dogs."

At this point, I wouldn't be surprised.

# CHAPTER TWO

"So do I get the grand tour?" I ask.

"There's not much to it. I opted for a studio instead of that atrocity of a mansion my father owns. Is that not the tackiest thing ever? It's like he's compensating for something, and if Stones are known for one thing...Well, we don't need to compensate for anything."

My knees weaken as he casually talks about being well-endowed. I'd love to find out how that confidence translates in the bedroom. But tacky? The Stone Mansion? Maybe he's confused. More like luxurious and awe-inspiring. But I suppose if that's what Devon grew up with, maybe he never found it to be home to him.

"Living room. Kitchen. I eat in both," he says. Then he nods toward the loft. "Up there's where I sleep and...partake in other extracurricular activities." He winks. "And there's a bathroom up there and down here. Pretty straightforward."

"And how many people know about your secret lair?" Translation: How many other girls do you bring here? How often? The idea of others standing right where I am...Never mind. I don't want to think about them.

"Not many. Consider yourself lucky."

I'd bet money he's just being nice.

He goes to the kitchen and pours us each a drink. Judging by the slowly tilting room, I'm not sure how much more alcohol I should consume tonight, but it's taking the edge off. I feel like I can do anything I want, and I'm pining to do Mr. Lust List Number Three.

Devon brings me another glass, this time red wine, and he walks past to sit on one of the leather couches. I follow, and he tosses aside the game controllers to make a spot for me. As soon as I sit, he reaches over and kisses me. His free hand grazes my shoulder and softly runs along one of my breasts. He moves his mouth to my neck, and the mix of his hot breath and smooth lips leaves me trembling.

"Not so fast there, killer," I say, pulling back. My own boldness catches me off guard. Maybe Devon's confidence is contagious, but as long as I feel I can speak my mind, then I'm going to try to uncover more of Devon. "You seem to have a lot of secrets. I don't know how I feel about all that."

"What do you want to know?" he asks, raising one eyebrow.

I hadn't thought that far ahead. "Um. How many...cars do you have?" Oh, what a dumb question.

"You think I'm hiding that from you like it's confidential information?"

"No," I laugh. "I need to stall while I think up something more specific." Something that'll teach me something about you that no one else knows.

"Four."

"Four?"

"Well, sort of. The Camaro is mine. It's the only one I care about." He draws little circles on my thigh as he speaks, and I have to contain my urge to giggle.

"And where is it?"

"Somewhere safe."

Right. "And the other three?"

"Those are Mark's responsibility. They're all leased. Two limos—one black, one white—and the Benz."

"Mhmm. You know how long I've had my run-down little Saturn?"

Devon gulps from his glass, draining it quickly. The sound of my own voice leaves me self-conscious, but I can't stop myself from jabbering on.

"Since the day I got my license. And it cost me two thousand dollars at a used car lot. That's six years, one car, no payments, and..." What am I doing talking about my lame car?

Devon smiles, but there's no sense of condescension at all. "I enjoy some of the benefits of being a Stone. I'm not going to pretend I don't. But it goes along with too much bullshit."

"Like what?" I ask.

"None of your concern." He places his empty glass on the coffee table, and I stare at the red bead of wine slowly dripping down the inside, settling at the bottom. "Tell me what life was like for you when you were ten."

I laugh, but he doesn't. Okay, this could be an interesting game. I imagine younger Devon was pretty wild, so if I divulge, he better too.

"Okay...um. Ten. I think that's the year my family went on a vacation to Disney World. We flew all the way to Florida to compare the World to the Land. But it was my first plane ride–*our* first, my brother's and mine–and our parents had to deal with us in a complete panic." It started with me crying, but then Jared took his big sister being upset to mean something was terribly wrong, so he joined in. I tell Devon all about our hysterics and how mom shut the window shades and made us pretend we were still on the ground. She was so patient with us that day. "We probably annoyed everyone on the plane, but how do you settle the fears of children who are certain they're about to die?" It should have been merely hypothetical, but my unfiltered mind jumped forward several years. How did Jared feel when he knew he was about to die?

I shake my head. No. Don't think about it. "Okay, your turn," I say. "Same question."

"When I was ten. My father took Kaidan and I down the red carpet of some event. Before then, we'd usually stay behind at the house with whichever nanny my dad was screwing at the time. But that year, he got us all dressed up in these stifling, stiff tuxedos and told us how no matter what, we had to hold our heads high and smile for the cameras. If we were asked questions, we had to be sure to give positive responses that made the business look good, and under no circumstances were we to talk about our personal lives."

"And how did that go? Did you hate the cameras back then too?"

"I've always hated the media, but I was up for an adventure. Plus, I had a plan." Devon relaxes back into the couch as he speaks, his head tilts back into the plush leather, and he closes his eyes. I follow the contours of his jaw to his chin over his Adam's apple, and I lick my lips. My mouth is suddenly very dry.

I sip at my wine and ask, "Which was?"

"To trip Kaidan halfway down the carpet."

"Oh, you did not!"

"Of course I did. And it went better than I could have ever planned. When we walk the red carpet, all the celebrities are perfectly spaced so the media can talk to everyone and the cameras have time to capture everybody. Ahead of us was that old band, Seventh Inferno, and when I stuck my foot out, Kaidan went flying. He toppled over and face-planted in front of everyone. The lead singer of Seventh Inferno was being interviewed at that same moment, so when it happened, everyone froze and zeroed in on Kaid. I swore he was going to piss himself."

"That's sort of mean, don't you think?" Only stating the obvious, of course.

"That's nothing compared to the crap we did to each other at home. Hell, the red carpet thing was payback from him dumping ice on me in the shower the week before and adding a bottle of women's perfume to my shampoo." Devon looks like he could fall asleep as he speaks, resting his eyes and speaking in a nonchalant tone, as if everyone experienced the same things growing up.

I could only imagine being the adult who had to wrangle these boys. "So that's what it's like to be a twin?"

"Or a Stone. Whether it's personal or business, it seems like everyone's always trying to one-up everyone else."

"Including you?" I ask.

He opens his eyes and looks at me, leaving several seconds of uncertainty before speaking. "Is that what you think I do?"

"Of course not." *Way to act like a jerk, O.* "Tell me what the infamous Stone twins were like at fifteen."

"Fifteen." He lifts my legs up onto his lap, and as he speaks he gently glides a hand up and down my shin. His touch sends chills up my spine, and I find myself getting distracted by his fingers. "I don't remember that much. We spent most our years fighting over girls, I do remember that."

"But who could possibly pass up that Devon charm?"

"That's what I've always said." He grins. "And they rarely did. Kaid's got his own tricks, though, I'm sure."

"And what are your tricks?" The room continues to spin, but all I can think about is how I love being this close to him. I love having him talk to me, openly and without other motives. This is a Devon I could easily fall for.

He leans forward and grabs ahold of my hips pulling me onto his lap. I help him out by straddling a leg on either side of him. My dress has hiked itself up and is showing off too much thigh, and Devon rubs his hands along both sides of me–up my thighs, along my hips, and underneath, gripping my butt. He pulls me toward him and kisses my stomach while staring up at me beneath my breasts. My fingers comb through his hair, and I sit back on his legs so I can reach his mouth. We kiss, and I swear the sparks between us could set the couch on fire.

His so-called tricks are the grand finale at a fireworks display. They're dynamite exploding every atom that makes up my being.

And then he cuts everything off, like a kid with an attention disorder. "Oh right!" Devon

says, sloppily pulling away from me. "I remember fifteen. We took my dad's car out for
a joy ride."

How can you get sidetracked from a kiss
like that? "You what?"

"We flipped for it to see who'd get to drive.
I called 'heads' and won."

"But you didn't even have a license back
then. That was il–" I cut myself off before
turning into Miss Obvious. Of course the le-
gality of it was not on their minds at fifteen.

"Dad had just gotten this hot, red Ferrari–
a little two-seater. We couldn't stay away
from it. He said if we even put a fingerprint
on it, we'd never see the light of day again."

"So you..."

"So we took it as a challenge and got three
miles away before crashing into a tree."

I gasp–such a ridiculous reaction, but I
couldn't help it. "What did he do?"

"Paid off the media to keep it out of the
headlines and bought himself a new one." He
says this so plainly, like it was the obvious so-

lution. At what point in your life is it normal to replace Ferarris like broken light bulbs?

"He let you guys get away with that?"

"It would've been too much effort to actually discipline us. But he did install a Devon-proof security system in the garage making it impossible to do it again–not that I didn't try."

"You're such a troublemaker," I say, kissing him again. "Why am I turned on by that?"

"Because I'm irresistible."

"You think so?" I gaze into his dark pupils. He's so certain of himself. Cocky but with every right.

"You tell me."

He runs a finger up my spine and over my jawline. My lips part, and I shiver. Tilting my head to one side, he leans up and kisses my neck. I arch my back and press myself into his lap even harder. I can feel my temperature rising as my heart flutters. I strain to keep my own composure. I want him, but I want more than sex. If this could lead to something more, then I don't want to be some one-night stand.

"Mhmm," I say, nodding. "Definitely irresistible."

He laughs and moves himself out from under me, standing up. "How about you? What was Olivia like at fifteen?" He walks back into the kitchen and pulls a beer from the fridge. His confidence and cool composure drive me crazy. "You want one?" he asks.

"No thanks." I try to think of life at fifteen while I wait for him to return. I'm sitting on the couch and smoothing my skirt back out when he speaks up again.

"Let me guess. Fifteen-year-old Olivia had straight As. She was actively involved in student government. She never missed a day and was every teacher's favorite student. I'm pretty close, right?"

I turn on the couch to face him. He's slowly pouring his beer into a glass. "*Actually*, Mr. Know-It-All. I smoked my first joint at fifteen."

The crashing of glass is satisfying as Devon is completely caught off guard by my confession. He's dropped the bottle, and amber shards lay in a puddle of beer on the floor.

I cover my mouth to keep from laughing, but I stand up in an attempt to help him clean the mess.

"You're either full of shit or full of surprises," Devon says.

He picks up the broken glass while I mop up the puddle. "Neither," I say. "That's about as *bad* as I ever got. Friends and I—we'd skip school and smoke pot in the woods. It's pretty juvenile." I glance over at him. His floor wasn't the only thing to fall victim to my confession. The bottom half of Devon's pants has two long lines of beer spilled down them. Now I feel bad.

He glances down and notices the mess on himself as well. He looks back up at me and says, "Maybe warn me next time."

"Sorry."

He walks past me and starts up the stairs to the second floor loft. He stops midway and looks back at me. "You coming?"

I follow him upstairs and am immediately met with an extra large bed, adorned in dark gray and black with a pile of pillows at the head of it. The headboard is black iron and curves around in a way that's threatening and alluring. This is a bed that looks like it has its own secrets. Two black side tables sit on either side of the bed. One has a book on it, the other, a lamp. Simple. I like that. A large, looming wardrobe is off on one side–its doors closed–and on top, a line of white candles. The fact that they're melted halfway down tells me someone else has been up here to enjoy them. To enjoy Devon. A coldness burrows through me, and my stomach does a flip. Jealousy.

But I'm here now. I need to forget Devon's less-than-appealing history, and that includes everyone in it. I turn away from the candles to see a doorway on the opposite wall. A bathroom. I step closer and see it's nearly as big as my bedroom. And where Devon's room was darker and a little on the gothic side, his bathroom is bright. White walls, huge mirrors, bright lighting...There's no hiding anything in there.

I stop in the doorway. Another door in here leads to his closet, and I can hear Devon inside. There's some rustling around and then he steps out.

*Thank you, god.*

He's naked. He's. Fucking. Naked. And here I thought I'd get some grand revealing at the right time. No. He ditched all his clothes and is now standing in front of me like it's no big deal.

But it is a big deal. Emphasis on the *big*.

I've already seen him shirtless, and that's a glorious view. But now? He's tan and toned. The outlines of his abs invite me closer. I want to trail my fingers along those crevices. I want to run my tongue along the even more defined indents above his hips that angle in, as if pointing toward the dark black curls of hair. My eyes follow, and as hard as I try to not look right at...him...my gaze betrays me and I find myself staring. Yeah, he's nice. Very nice. In my mind, visions race through of me gripping him in my hands. Him thrusting into me. Me holding onto the headboard of his bed as he has his way with me.

"You're blushing." He interrupts my happy thoughts and walks past me out of the bathroom. He briskly strides to his wardrobe, pulls out a pair of boxer briefs, and steps into them. I'm trying to think of something–anything–to say to ease the tension building up in me. Devon walks back to his closet, and a moment later, he's back out wearing a pair of flannel pants and no shirt. I want to wake up to this relaxed version of him forever.

"So tell me more about Pothead Olivia."

"Ugh...no. That's not who I was at all. I was young and experimenting."

"*Experimenting*. I like the sound of that." Devon walks into his room and flops down onto his bed. He relaxes into the plush mattress, one leg outstretched, the other bent at the knee.

"Then it must still sound more exciting than it was. I spent more time hiding from my parents and bribing Jared not to tell on me than I did doing the things that would get me in trouble."

"Who's Jared? An old boyfriend?"

My stomach turns, and I realize I'd kept myself from saying his name before. I sit on the edge of Devon's bed. "My—um—my brother."

"You said he died. What happened?"

No one ever asked me that so bluntly. Usually, people avoided bringing it up altogether. Even right after he died, some of my friends carried on acting like nothing happened at all. No one's lives had changed. No one's lives had been turned upside down. Yet, Devon openly asks.

"He was being bullied. One day, they...took it too far. They beat him until he was unconscious." I can feel my eyes welling up with tears. "Only, he never woke up."

"Shit. That's bad." There's a sense of shock in his eyes, even if he doesn't have the right things to say to make me feel better. "What happened to the guys that did it?"

"They were only kids. They were charged as kids. They..." My chest is tightening. Flashes of anger flood through me, and I can't bring myself to say more. "Can we not talk about it?"

I feel tears running down my cheek as Devon sits up straight and reaches out for me.

"Hey, hey." He takes my hands and pulls me toward him. I settle in next to him, my head on his chest, my legs tangled with his.

Dammit. I had expectations for tonight, and none of them involved me crying in Devon's bedroom.

# CHAPTER THREE

The gentle lull of his heartbeat settles my mind. The rushing thoughts of past memories, of the loss my family endured, how we never recovered—they taper off and slow as I find myself hypnotized by the thumping of his heart, the steady rise and fall of his chest, and the warmth and security of his arms encircling me. My eyes feel too heavy to keep open, so I give into temptation and let myself get lost on the serene wave of Devon.

"You're so haunted," Devon says to me, his voice soft and low. How can somebody who himself is filled with trouble and secrets be such a comfort to me? "What's it going to take to make you happy?"

"You make me happy," I mumble.

He disregards my compliment. "What do you want for yourself?"

I think about it. Life's like a checklist, right? I moved away from home, went to college, graduated. "I want to be an event planner. You know, coordinate the things that bring people their best memories." Particularly when my own memories aren't as great.

"That's a job. That's not what I was asking. You really think that would make you feel fulfilled when you're lying on your deathbed?"

I give it some consideration. I mean, if I'm being perfectly honest, "I'd find some way to change the world."

He laughs, his outburst jolting me out of my own exhaustion, but he stops himself quickly. "Sorry. You caught me off guard. Now you're being too broad. How are you going to change the world, Wonder Woman?"

It feels like another life, but before everything happened with Jared, I remember how
my family was. Dad was trying to move up in
politics. He'd succeeded after he left his family behind. Now he was a senator up in Wash-
ington. When they were together, mom
helped him. She was involved in a bunch of
nonprofits, and they were like the perfect
team. If our family hadn't fallen to ruins, who
knows what they could have accomplished? I
never took it seriously as a kid. Politics
seemed dull. But now...

"I'd get involved in activism. Equal
rights...gay marriage and..." I yawn. "I'd get
involved with schools. You know, help shape
the younger generation, so there's less hate
and intolerance as they get older." I'd stand
up for those who are bullied or hurt–
something I should've done five years ago.

Devon nods his head. "Admirable. I'll buy
you a cape. Where does the passion come
from though?"

"My brother was gay." My breath catches. I can't believe I admitted that so easily. I don't think I've ever said it out loud. "Wow."

"Were you not supposed to tell me that or something?"

"No. I–uh–I've always kept it to myself. He told me right before. He didn't get a chance to tell anyone else. That moment was the closest we'd been in a long time." I take a deep breath. It's painful to talk about it, but strangely, it feels lightening confiding in Devon. "And then he was gone."

"Why didn't you tell people after, *for* him?"

"After? Because I was a mess. My family was a mess. My parents were burdened with guilt. He'd been complaining about being bullied, but dad told him to suck it up and fight back. After..." I stop speaking to relax my breathing and my rampaging thoughts. "After he died, rumors were going around. Only they weren't rumors, obviously. But only I knew that. My parents refused to believe them, and I wasn't in a state of mind to correct them. I didn't care about them. I didn't care about anything. Then dad moved out. I haven't seen him much since. Mom stopped speaking for a while. And I counted down the days to when I could move away and start a new life."

Is it me, or is it entirely too late at night to be talking like this? But the sound of Devon's voice soothes me. "It seems like that past followed you though." He's not afraid to speak the truth. I admire that.

And he's right. The OCD, the walls I put up. I never did start that new life.

"It's alright, Olivia. You'll save the world. You've got plenty of time."

"And what about you?" I ask. "What are you going to do?" Which reminds me... "What did you find out about your dad's will? You went through all that trouble, yet..."

"I haven't looked at it yet. I'll get around to it."

Self-restraint? That's impressive. "Don't you think he'll notice it's gone?"

"It doesn't matter."

"But you have it now. You can find out what you were wondering. You have your answers yet you aren't in any rush to see them?" I feel like I'm mumbling nonsense as I fight to stay awake.

He gives a soft laugh. "Often. The answers don't bring any resolve. I'm right where I want to be right now. What's in that envelope won't make anything better. So I'll leave it."

And again he makes life seem so effortless. It's me and him, lying together in his bed as he lures me to sleep with his steady breathing and firm, warm body. He acts like things are so easy.

Ignore the bad stuff. Bask in the good.

Do what you want. When you want.

Push away all the negativity. All the guilt. All the demons of memories past...

*"Can I talk to you?"*

*Jared waltzes into my room, unannounced, again. This kid has no clue what privacy means. I give him a dirty glare and turn away, my phone still pressed to my ear.* "Tyler, Jared just burst in thinking his time's more important than anyone else's. Can I call you back?"

"Yeah, whatever. I'm probably gonna be gone though."

*Tyler and I are almost a year into our relationship. At seventeen-years-old, that's record-breaking for me. We're like an old, married couple at this point. We even call each other "Mr." and "Mrs.". I'd be lying if I said I hadn't planned out some of the details of our eventual wedding.*

"Wait. I thought you said you weren't going out with them." *He wants to hang out with the group, but there's a new girl infiltrating it, Kelsey, and I don't like how she flirts with Tyler. Since I'm grounded for breaking curfew, I made him promise he wouldn't hang around her.*

"Relax. Nothing's going to happen. And if you hadn't gotten in trouble, you'd be coming with. So I'll just pretend you're there, 'kay?"

I hardly feel better. He loves the attention he's getting from her. I can tell.

I hang up with Tyler and sigh as I turn back to my annoying little brother.

"What?" I snap.

He takes another step into my room and closes the door behind him. "You might want to sit."

"Don't be so dramatic. Tell me whatever it is so you can leave me alone."

I sulk to my bed. Pissed that I'm grounded and pissed that I don't know what Tyler will be doing tonight. But he loves me. He told me so.

"Okay, well," Jared starts, "you know how... Or–um...Well, my friend, Rhys. You know him."

"You mean Reese's Pieces? Of course, I know him. He's only been your best friend since you were in kindergarten." Must be *nice. I don't think I have any friends I've known that long. But Jared and Rhys are inseparable, like the brother he never had.*

*"Right. So...uh."*

*"Dude. Spit it out." He's being more obnoxious than usual.*

*Jared inhales a deep breath and spits out the next line as fast as he can, his eyes closed. "Don't tell mom and dad, but Rhys is my boyfriend now. Like, we're–we're a couple. Like you and Tyler."*

*His shoulders drop like he's released a two hundred-pound barbell.*

*And my reaction is one hundred percent genuine.*

*I burst out laughing. "You're so full of shit."*

*Jared gay? Right. He's only a freshman but already on the junior varsity baseball team. He isn't some feminine kid in drama club.*

*"Why would I lie about this?" he asks. His face is firm and serious.*

"*Because you're bored. You're trying to mess with me. Now go away.*"

*Instead of leaving my room, he walks to my bed and sits down next to me. He really can't take a hint.*

"*I like guys,*" *he says, looking me straight in the eye.* "*No one knows. Only you. And Rhys.*"

"*I don't believe you. There's nothing gay about you–*"

"*You think there's some flashing sign that goes off near gay people?*" *Now he sounds defensive. Shit. Maybe he's being serious.* "*Gay people are just like you. Just like everyone. You know what is gay about me? The fact I have a boyfriend.*"

"*Why are you telling me this?*"

*We weren't exactly close. We'd been at each other's necks for years. As little kids, we were best friends, but somewhere around puberty, our bond had dissolved.*

"*I don't know who else I can go to. I thought you'd be understanding, open.*"

*Thanks for trying to make me feel guilty.*

*I comb my fingers through my hair. This week, I have pink streaks in it. "Sorry. Wow."*

*I'm pretty speechless.*

*"Please don't tell mom and dad."*

*"They'd freak," I say.*

*"I know. So promise." There's a sense of desperation in his voice.*

*"I promise." How long has it taken him to even come to me? How long has he known and been hiding it? I think to all the times I've seen him with Rhys. No one could have ever guessed. I feel a sudden sadness imagining being in his position.*

*If he thought he could trust me, then I'll be someone he can trust.*

*"They won't find out," I confirm. "They won't find out."*

# CHAPTER FOUR

*Find out.*

"Find out who the fuck this is, now." Someone is shouting. "... I don't care how long it takes. It's your goddamn job ... Privacy my ass, just find out."

My eyes jolt open. It's morning, and I don't know where I am. A strange bed. A strange room. A strange voice, yelling. My heart almost leaps through my chest as I sit up in a panic. Where am I?

My hazy mind starts to clear, and things begin to make sense. Devon. I'm in his room.

In his condo. He's the one yelling. I reach for my phone right as I remember I don't have it. It's okay. You're okay, O. I climb out of bed and stumble to the railing of his upstairs loft. The floor seems to tilt and shift under my feet. Devon's down in the living room, pacing, with his phone to his ear. His shoulders are squared off and tense. I can't help but gaze at his bare chest. Why did I have to get all emotional last night? We'd gone from steamy potential to Devon soothing my troubled mind to sleep. And now he's in a fury on the phone. Who's he talking to?

I lean into the cool, metal rails trying to focus on the real world, but my mind returns to the vivid memories that have taken over my dreams for years. I'd kept my promise to Jared. I never told. My parents never knew...until the rumors started. Then they argued about the validity. Mom said it didn't matter. Dad said it was preposterous. He didn't have a gay son. He'd never allow that. Mom cried because they didn't have a son at all anymore. I stayed out of it all. Like Devon told me last night, the truth wasn't going to fix anything. It wouldn't get better.

No, stop thinking about it. Five years ago, and it was still a fresh wound. I take a deep breath pushing out the bad thoughts, and as they drift away, a pounding headache settles in the vacant space. Perfect. A hangover, a nightmare, and a bad ending to a promising night.

I stare down at Devon whose disheveled hair makes me smile. He's pacing barefoot across the living room floor clenching his fist as he speaks to whoever is on the phone. I stand up straighter intending to go down and meet him, but the headache knocks against my brain harder, and my stomach tightens. It's suddenly hot in here, and each inhale makes my throat constrict.

I'm going to be sick.

I rush to Devon's bathroom, slamming the door shut and locking it. Please don't come up here now. I throw myself toward the toilet in time to empty the contents of my stomach. That's what I get for drinking so much and eating so little.

I sit on the cold tile floor, last night's dress now wrinkled and out of place. I couldn't feel trashier if I tried. After a minute, I force myself to stand, flush the toilet, and wash my hands. I open the medicine cabinet hoping to find mouthwash and succeed. While swishing the minty liquid around my mouth and focusing on my breathing to ease the sick feeling in my stomach, I notice the medicine cabinet is well stocked... Condoms next to the Tylenol. Warming lotion next to dental floss. And multiple orange bottles with unidentifiable pills inside. Prescriptions... for what?

Listening intently, I can hear the threatening tone in Devon's muffled voice as he continues his conversation. He's still downstairs, so I grab the only bottle that still has a label and read what I can make out of the dirty, faded text.

*L Shel*

Who's that? Why does Devon have someone else's prescription? What are these for? Looking at the label on this one, it's hard to not jump to conclusions.

Vicodin.

I check another bottle and read the imprinted name on the round pills. Percocet.

And a third bottle. Valium.

Are they all meant for this "L Shel" person? I'm not an idiot. It's illegal for him to have these. And it's stupid. Hell, there are reports, practically weekly, of high-profile people losing their lives after mixing prescriptions.

A knock on the door and I almost drop the bottle I'm holding. I silently replace it and close the medicine cabinet door. "Yeah?" I ask.

"You okay?"

I check myself in the mirror, attempt to fix my hair, and wipe away the smudged makeup under my eyes. "Yeah, I'm fine." I take a deep breath as I try to believe my own words. My hands shake, and I swallow back a number of arguments.

I walk to the door and open it to find Devon standing in the middle of his room, clutching his phone in his hand. He's still pissed. And so am I. How can someone like him be so...so stupid about his own wellbeing? But for now, Devon's rage clearly surpasses my own frustration.

"Are you okay?" I ask. Also, what the hell's up with the drug store in your bathroom?

"I opened the will."

"Oh?" My stomach's doing backflips while a marching band drums on my brain, so I go back to his bed to sit down. "I take it you were right? Your dad wrote you out of it?"

"Not exactly. He intends to leave me with much less than I expected–though I shouldn't be surprised–but considering he's probably going to outlive all of us, none of that will matter any time soon. No, there was something weird in it. There's a request in it to 'continue transferring $5,000 every month to

M. H. of Bandon, Oregon'. Now, why does some stranger need $60,000 a year from my father? And how long has he been paying this person?"

"So you want to know who it is?" Maybe another time I'd find all this exciting. Instead, I'm distracted by the questions I have now and how to approach Devon with them. He's already angry, and I'm not sure I want to deal with his wrath.

"Damn right I do. Obviously, he's made some sort of deal. What info does he have that he's hiding? My dad's paid plenty of people off through the years. But no one has seen a regular payout like this. Especially not one that'll continue when he dies."

"So how do you find out? And how do you know it's a guy?"

"I don't, but my private investigator has till the end of the day to get me something."

His private investigator? "Why do you have a—"

"Long story. Want some coffee?"

I guess that's the end of that. "Yes. Please."

He walks downstairs, and I scoop my heels up off the floor next to his bed and follow slowly behind him, glancing back at the bathroom door as it disappears from my view. By the bottom step, I'm feeling woozy. Deep breaths.

"On second thought. Maybe I should get going."

"What's your rush? I've got nothing going on today. You?"

I take a seat at a bar stool in his kitchen. "Aside from the ongoing search for employment?"

"Right, you quit. Wish I'd been there to see it."

"It wasn't impressive." Well, maybe it was for me.

"You should give yourself more credit."

I shrug my shoulders. How am I supposed to believe him when he's hiding things from me? Is this how it'll always be?

"How do you like your coffee?"

"Strong. With cream and sugar." I can't keep ignoring the elephant in the medicine cabinet. Small talk is only making it more stressful. I breathe in slowly, willing myself to relax and say something. Anything. "I need to ask you something."

He brings a mug to me and nods toward the couch. "Sit. Drink."

I don't know if he's ignoring me or if he didn't hear. "No."

"What?"

I grip the steaming mug, letting the heat seep into my palms. "I'm sorry. I was in your bathroom earlier. I saw the...I saw the pills." There, I said it. Now it's up to him to explain himself.

"You snooped through my things?" An annoyed scowl crosses his face.

That's not the point. Doesn't he at least feel ashamed? I'm not going to let him turn this around on me.

"I needed something, so I looked in the most logical place." I look away from his cold glare. "I didn't mean to find anything–I mean, I didn't expect to see illegal—"

Devon bursts out laughing and rolls his eyes. "It must be great being you–such a law-abiding good girl." He walks over to me and drinks his coffee as if we're having a leisurely chat. He looks me right in the eye and says, "I bet your story about skipping school–experimenting, as you claimed–was all bull-shit, wasn't it?"

"No, Devon," I argue. My hands are shaking so bad I have to put my mug on a table to keep from burning myself. "I'm not the liar here."

He lowers his voice, and the room seems to grow colder. "Are you saying I am?"

"Why are they in your bathroom?" My voice shakes.

"It's none of your goddamn business. How's that for an answer?"

I have to get out of here. If he'd rather fight and be cruel than explain himself and clear my worries, then why am I here? What

is there for us if Devon's only going to continue hiding himself from me?

My stomach aches, and my head spins. "I
need to go home."

"You're really going to make a big deal
about this." He shakes his head.

I stand firm, my arms crossed in front of
me. I'm barely keeping it together. My legs
feel weak, and I want to scream. But on the
outside, I try to appear as confident and unre-
lenting as Devon.

He pulls his phone out and turns away
from me.

"Mark. Come pick up Olivia and see she
gets home."

A few seconds later, he hangs up and looks
back at me. "Down the elevator and out the
doors on the right. He'll meet you out front."
And with that, he goes upstairs, and I hear
the bathroom door slam shut.

My body trembles as I strap my heels on
and hurry out. During the elevator ride down
I breathe back my own tears unsuccessfully,

finally giving in and letting the stress take control of me. The doors open at the ground floor, and I wipe my eyes as I follow Devon's directions and leave through the doors.

But I didn't expect to walk straight into a gym—an open gym. Filled with dozens of men working out and lifting weights and toweling sweat from their faces. And every one of them turns toward me as I push through the doors and make my way to the exit. I can feel my face turn beet red. Here you see a random girl, in yesterday's fancy gown, interrupting your workout routine. Never mind the smeared makeup or the fact I'm about to have a panic attack. Carry on. I cross my arms in front of me, digging my nails into my skin. I'm okay. Just need to walk faster. The sound of heavy metal clanging against more heavy metal makes me jump, and I break out in a sweat as I rush through the glass doors and out into the open air. As promised, Mark waits at the curb. I jump in the back, tell him my address, and settle against the leather seats, my gaze focused on the sights outside. I feel sick and guilty. Like I screwed up in a major way. I doubt his other girlfriends have ever had a problem with Devon's secrets. But I'm not them. I don't know if I could ever be them.

# CHAPTER FIVE

We pull up to my apartment complex, and I couldn't be more relieved. I feel like a fool having to knock on the door of my own home, but that's what I get for ditching my stuff in my glorious act of boldness last night.

Last night.

It feels like it happened weeks ago. One week with Devon—one night with him—and my entire life feels like it's not my own.

I bang on the door again, more persistent this time.

I hear rushed steps and a sing-song voice from inside. "Walk of shame. Walk of shame," Maddie's singing to me, and I can only wish I had sexier news to share.

The door swings open to reveal my too-excited roommate wrapped in a sheet, grinning from ear to ear.

"I have to say," she starts, "I couldn't be more proud of you."

"What are you talking about?" I go to push past her, but she embraces me in an awkward hug instead.

"Careful, you're going to lose your cover." As long as it took her to answer the door, she could have thrown on some clothes. I walk in and survey the living room. "Please tell me you grabbed my purse. I left it next to yours."

"It's in your room, but let's not pretend nothing happened. Spill it, girl. I want details."

I ignore her. The truth is disappointing. She'd be much happier hearing about a wild night of naked shenanigans. I walk into my room, but she follows. My purse lies in the middle of my still-made-up bed. The comforter is free from wrinkles just like I left it yesterday. I can't think of the last time I was out all night. It makes the image of my untouched bed that much stranger.

"So what was he like? Sweet and gentle? Or rough and dirty? I bet he's the rough and dirty type. And a Mr. VIP on top of it."

"Mr. What?" I pull my phone out of my purse only to find it dead, so I plug it in as Maddie continues rambling. I walk to my closet and throw on jeans and a tank top, discarding my pretty dress on the floor.

"VIP. Very Impressive Penis. You really don't stay up-to-date on *ScandalLust* do you? I think it originated at LUSH. I swear so many trends come out of that club, yet I can never get *in*." She bounces onto my bed still clutching the sheet and looking like she's on her way to a toga party. "It's true, right? The VIP status?"

As a matter of fact...But it's not like I'm going to tell her that. My phone blinks back to life with a voicemail waiting for me. The perfect excuse not to explain last night to Maddie, I lean down so my charging phone can reach my ear.

"This message is for Olivia Margot. My name is Robert Klein. I'm calling from Eco-Groove Events. We're very interested in having you in for an interview. We have several employment opportunities available and are certain you'd be an excellent fit. Please call back at..."

I listen to the rest and then play it over again. Weird. How'd they even get my number?

"...Leave your best friend hanging, when all I want to do is celebrate your liberation." Maddie's been talking this whole time. She's far too excited. "You realize the step you took last night? I mean, for an ordinary person, promiscuity is no big deal, but you...You, Liv, are *extra*ordinary. You–"

"Are you sure you're not putting all the attention on me because you don't want to tell me about *your* night?" I leave my room and head toward the bathroom to brush my teeth. Maddie follows.

"My night?" Maddie says, leaning against the doorframe. "I cleaned the bar. Packed away glasses and bottles. Came home. Showered. Went to bed. What are you not telling me?"

"Nothing," I snap. "I need to lie down. Sorry. We'll talk more later, okay?" I head back toward my room. This time Maddie doesn't follow.

"Are you alright?" she asks, and I look back at her to see her face wrinkled with worry.

There's no easy way to answer that. "I will be."

I close the door behind me and fall, defeated, into my bed. Squeezing my eyes shut, I try to forget everything that happened this morning—and last night, for that matter.

Maybe I'm not cut out for the Hollywood life. But there has to be more to Devon. He's not letting me in, and I can accept that. It's only been a week. But underneath the anger and defensiveness, there has to be another side to him. I've seen it in the fleeting moments where he's been sweet and gentle and thoughtful. I want to be the one to bring out the *real* Devon Stone.

But he has to want that as well.

I wake up feeling groggy a couple hours later and stumble out to the kitchen to try to start the day over again with a fresh pot of coffee. The TV's on, and I'm surprised to see Maddie has company. I do a double take as I realize that, though she's managed to get dressed, this guy is relaxing in my living room–on my couch–in his boxers. I recognize him too. He's the hot blond guy with a lip ring Maddie was talking to at the party. I glare at her until her eyes meet mine, and she can't help but smile.

She jumps up and comes over to me. "How are you feeling?"

"Fine," I say. "So you came home, showered, and went to bed? You liar."

She grins wildly and points her finger at me, lowering her voice to a whisper. "Hey, I didn't say a single thing that wasn't true. I just didn't do any of those things *alone*."

"Mhmm."

We both laugh, and Maddie returns to her new friend. I settle into the loveseat as Maddie introduces us.

"Olivia, this is Corey. Corey, Olivia."

He nods and then his eyes light up like he's realized something.

"I know you," he says.

"You do?" Please don't tell me he reads tabloids too.

"Devon's girl."

"So you know Devon?"

"Sort of. Not really." Okay, this guy's not lacking in the looks department, but I'm far from impressed with his conversational skills.

"My cousin's a friend of his. Well, was. They got in trouble a while back. I don't think they talk much anymore."

Why doesn't that surprise me? It seems like Devon's entire past revolves around the theme of 'Trouble'. "What sort of trouble did they get into?" I'm sure I could guess with limited tries. Drugs? Burglary? Reckless driving? Or something all new like hiring a prostitute or...

"They trashed a hotel after a gig one night."

What? That's it? That's not even criminal—just...rude. "I'm sorry, elaborate a little?"

"Parasyt—with a 'y'—had a gig, opening for Tempest Ultra a few years ago."

"Who's Parasyt?"

Now he talks to me like I'm slow. "Your boyfriend's band. Old band, I guess. They haven't done much recently."

Hold the fucking phone. Devon is—was—in a band? I laugh, imagining him on a stage in front of an adoring audience.

"You don't believe me."

I may have only recently met Devon, but something tells me I'd know if the son of the biggest international record label had his own band. I mean, it's not like they'd have trouble getting signed. Calvin Stone could snap his fingers and make them the biggest band in the world. "Of course I believe you." *Or hardly at all, buddy.*

My laptop lays on a side table, and I pull it over to me and open it to do my own digging. If it's true, I can certainly find it, but my expectations are pretty low.

"They finished a decent set, and then had some insane afterparty at the hotel."

I type in a search for Parasyt that immediately tries to correct to the proper spelling. But below the unhelpful "Did you mean...", there are results listed, the most recent being over two years ago. The title reads, *Sex, Drugs, Rock and Roll–Have Devon Stone and Kennedy Rose gone from touring pals to...something more?*

I curl my lip in faint disgust, remembering how nasty Kennedy was last night. Wonder how she's doing right now...It might be cruel, but her disappointment makes me a little giddy.

The next result sounds like it could be something. *When Rock Stars Get Rowdy.*

I click it, and a page opens to some indie rock blog–dark and edgy colors and fonts and a big photo at the top of Devon behind a drum kit. This might be the best revelation about him yet. In the picture, he's in a grungy club, drenched in sweat, holding two drumsticks, looking like he's out to kill a cymbal rather than set the rhythm. His bandmates are on the stage in front of him decked out in eyeliner and head-to-toe black ensembles.

Corey continues to ramble on about unimportant details, claiming his cousin told him so, while I fact check and try to hide my amusement. Devon in a band. All the attention he says he hates.

But then I read the article. Sure, like cliché rock stars they messed up the hotel room, broke a mirror and stained the bathtub blue with an impromptu hair dying session–I bet Kennedy was involved in that. But it's not the liquor bottles or pot smoke smell they left behind that's unsettling. It's the pill bottles that were later found. *Damn.*

All my anger from earlier comes back. This isn't some minor misunderstanding. This is bigger than that. I had every right to ask Devon, and the fact he fought with me and wouldn't talk about it...A pit in my stomach confirms something isn't right.

I have the urge to tell Maddie everything. She always has the right solutions. But with company...

There's a knock at the door, and Maddie leaps up to answer. No, I'll have to talk to her later. She clearly has plans today. I don't want to bring her down.

I'm staring at the computer screen when I hear, "Olivia."

My heart stops, and I look up. Devon is standing in the doorway.

# CHAPTER SIX

Devon strolls in and surveys the place as he walks toward me. Maddie's wide eyes follow him, and I stand up, leaning down to quickly shut my laptop. It's a surreal moment for sure–having Hollywood royalty in our crummy apartment. Devon approaches me, and I don't know what to say.

"Hey." That's the best I've got right now. I'm too surprised he's even here.

"Hey man," Corey echoes, clearly unfazed by the fact he's in his underwear, surrounded by people.

Devon gives him a quick once over and scrunches up his face at the sight of the half-naked guy. But he doesn't seem to recognize him. He looks back at me. "Can we talk? Privately?"

Maddie grabs Corey's hand and pulls him toward her room. "We'll get out of your way."

I know her tricks. These walls are paper-thin. It wouldn't matter where we went, she'd be able to hear everything.

Once we have the room to ourselves, Devon speaks quietly. "I'm leaving," he says.

"You just got here."

"I'm going away for a couple days. To Oregon."

So he's really on a mission to find this M. H. person? "Did your guy call you back? What did he find out?"

"A load of worthless shit. I'm going to have to do this myself." He grazes his hand over my arm, and I flinch. I step back from him.

"Why are you here telling me this?"

"Because I want you to go with me." He runs his hand through his hair as though we're in high school, and he's nervously waiting for me to accept his invitation to prom.

But where's all this coming from? He was pissed at me earlier. We fought. I left. How can he come here acting like none of that happened? Why would I run off with him again now?

He can't pretend everything is okay between us. "I have plans tomorrow...I can't—"

"I'm sorry I was an asshole earlier." He speaks quickly, spitting out his words as though he hates the sound of them.

I wait for him to continue.

"The pills you found are my friend's. Lucas's. Lucas *Shelton* if you paid any attention to what was written on the bottle. You met him on the yacht, remember?"

L Shel. Lucas Shelton.

Tattooed, pierced Lucas who thought Devon getting caught with a stolen car while having sex with his ex was hilarious. Yeah, I remember him, and my skin crawls thinking of him.

"He was staying at my place for a while. He left them behind and hasn't come back for them yet. Last I checked, it's not my job to play housekeeper, so if he wants them, he knows where to find them."

"So they aren't yours?" I rub my stomach, trying to settle the uneasy feeling that persists.

"Is my name Lucas?"

I drop my defenses, letting my arms relax. "Why does Lucas have all of them?"

"Those are his issues to deal with. You'll have to ask him."

Yeah right. That guy gave me weird vibes on the yacht. I'd rather not see him again.

"Why couldn't you tell me that this morning?"

"Because I'm not a fan of being attacked in my own place, especially by nosy girlfriends."

Talk about mixed reactions. I don't know whether to smack him or kiss him. Did he just call me his girlfriend, insulting me in the same sentence?

"I'm not sure a road trip is the answer to our problems." I can only imagine. Me. Devon. Hours of arguing. That would be the end of us entirely. Without a doubt.

Devon closes the space between us and kisses me. "I said I was sorry. Come with me." He wraps his arms around my waist, pulling me closer. Kissing my ear, his lips send shivers through my entire body. "Think," he whispers, and my breath catches in my throat, "the two of us. All alone. For days." He speaks low, and I close my eyes. "We can do anything we want."

I snap out of his trance and step back. "You mean days of us arguing and you losing your temper?" I add a quick smile so he knows I'm not being completely serious. But really, that's what I can predict. This trip can go really great... or it can backfire like a nightmare.

Devon looks down on me, his eyes intently focused on mine. "I'll be on my best behavior."

He's intoxicating. Looking at him puts me under his spell. "Well, let's not go *that* far." Maybe I *want* a taste of Devon's trouble. And I really don't have anything better to do. "I'd need to pack. I'm not sure I even have a bag..."

As quickly as I say it, Maddie's door opens, and a pink duffel bag comes flying out, landing at my feet. Of course she was eavesdropping. Her door closes without us catching a glimpse of her, and I laugh. "All right then. Give me a minute."

I take the bag to my room and drop it onto my bed. I'm not sure this is a good idea, and my body seems to agree. My stomach turns at the thought of leaving town, and my hands tremble. I convince myself it's merely excitement. I take a deep breath. This will be fun—I hope. But if anything's going to happen between me and Devon, then I have to take some risks.

I unzip the duffel bag and pull it open to find my trusty best friend has provided her own contributions. I stifle my laughter as I inventory a tiny red dress, black lacy lingerie, and a sealed sample bottle of edible massage oil. She even included a few condoms. *Maddie to the rescue.* I feel my cheeks redden, and then my heart jolts at the sound of footsteps from behind. I jam everything back into the bag right as Devon walks into my room. I hide my embarrassed face as I rush through my closet and drawers picking out the best of what I have.

"So...why do you even want to find this person?" Is it really necessary? I feel like it won't make him feel any better to meet the guy in his father's will.

Devon leans against my desk, picking up my worn out copy of *Jane Eyre*. Now there's a girl who can take control. "My dad's gotten into...situations...in the past." He ruffles through some pages and sets the book back down. "This looks like another, so I want to know for sure."

"Can't your private investigator find out?" I pile my clothes into the bag while watching Devon.

"He hasn't found anything yet. Leaving now, we'll have a head start for when he does."

I pack my phone charger and makeup and pick up the bag to carry it to the bathroom.

"I'll help you," Devon says, coming over to me.

"It's okay. I got it." On the way to the bathroom I ask, "For someone who doesn't get along with his family at all, why do you care so much?" I finish packing and we return to the living room.

"My family in a nutshell–they'd rather use money to solve their problems. I think that's bullshit. Therefore, I'm the only one who actually gets anything fixed."

"Even after the way they treat you?" Screwing him over with the company. Taking away his inheritance. The blatant insults...

"I'm not doing it for them," he snaps.

But I don't believe him. I drop it, since I know challenging him will only lead to another fight. If he's not doing it for his family, then why are we going? For Devon? For his pride? His curiosity. No. This is to protect those he loves the most, whether he'll admit it or not.

# CHAPTER SEVEN

Devon's sporty blue Camaro glistens in the sunlight in the parking lot of my apartment complex. I could almost convince myself he cleans and waxes it everyday, but I'm sure he has staff for that.

"So where to first, Mr. Stone?"

"We'll know when we get there." Devon flashes me his sexy smile and takes my bag, tossing it in the trunk next to his own. He drops into the driver's side seat and waits for me to get in. I sit down and barely have my second leg inside when Devon switches to reverse and hits the gas. The car jolts backward as I yank my foot in and pull the door shut. He shifts gears again and takes off like we're in a car chase fleeing the scene of a crime. I buckle my seatbelt and hug my purse in my lap as we pull out onto the road. Who knows what I've gotten myself into this time?

The relentless L.A. traffic prevents us from getting out of town too fast. While Devon does his best to weave through the lanes of cars, narrowly missing semis and flipping off motorcyclists who are even riskier than he is, the breeze coming through his open window wages war on his messy hair. The dark locks blow across his forehead, and mixed with his intense focus on the road and the scruff on his unshaven face, it's really hard to look away.

He catches me staring. "What?" He glances over for a split second.

"Oh nothing. I read something about you..."

"More snooping? Should I hire *you* as my private investigator?"

I feel my skin flush. "It's not that." Well, yes it is, but, "Corey–the guy at the apartment with Maddie–"

"I know who he is." His eyes stay on the road, and he seems hardly interested in what Corey had to say.

"He mentioned you were in a band."

Devon snarls his top lip like he smelled something awful. "You couldn't have nosed around for something better?"

I laugh. "How can anything be better than rock star Devon, drummer for Parasyt–spelled wrong?"

"It wasn't a big deal. Just some shitty garage band. It's not like we hit the charts or anything." He runs a hand through his hair as if that marks the end of the discussion, but I only have loads of questions.

"But why? You could have I'm sure." You know...connections and all that. Daddy Stone should have been able to pull some strings.

"You mean we could've signed to Stone? No thanks. I didn't want it to be a job. It was for fun. Once you become a label slave, it loses its appeal."

"I don't know. I've seen rock stars on TV and stuff. They're pretty happy with their success."

"Good actors. They're riding the high that comes with money and attention. I've seen it often. They trade happiness for a song. I might not be very career-focused right now, but at least I still have my identity. That's far more important than anything a hit single could provide."

Tell me how you really feel, Devon.

Maybe he's right. Maybe I know nothing about this world. And yet, I'm a part of it now. I'll have to learn. It's amazing when you think about it. In this past week, my life has completely changed. I took a leap and landed right here—next to a man I couldn't have thought up in my dreams if I tried. Even being rough around the edges, Devon is infinitely better than any boyfriend from my past. Take my last boyfriend, Bryce, for example. I may have pushed him away in fear he was developing a gambling addiction, but if I think about it, there were far more reasons I should have dumped him earlier than I did. He'd spend days lounging on my sofa in his pajamas playing video games. He claimed to have a part-time job, but I never saw him go to it. The only time he'd get dressed and leave was when he was spending the weekend in Vegas with friends. Then he was suddenly some sophisticated, suit-wearing top dog. Granted, I think it was him in those suits that kept me around–I love a man who cleans up well–but the reality is, it was easy to be with him. I wasn't challenged. I didn't have to do anything outside my comfort zone. Things were safe...and really fucking boring.

But Devon. Good god, Devon couldn't be more opposite. Unpredictable, adventurous, and determined. Like now, he only has vague information to work off of, yet we're driving out of state for the possibility of an answer that'll lead to...what?

I feel a knot in my stomach as I remember this isn't exactly a vacation. What we find out in Oregon, it can lead to even more trouble. And then what? I'll be right there with Devon to take on that trouble. There won't be any- where for me to run when–*if*–things get out of hand.

"So. M. H.," I say. "You don't know anyone with those initials?"

"Not that I know of. No one that matters, at least. I'm sure there's a million people that it can be, but...all I've got right now is a hunch." He slams on his brakes and the horn at the same time as a car cuts us off, yet his voice remains calm and sure. "We'll figure it out up there."

"What hunch?" He knows more? Why didn't he say so?

"It's only a theory," he says. "I don't want to talk about it. Not until I have proof."

And the plot thickens with Mr. Stone. If he's not going to share the details, then we, at least, need a plan. Nothing gets done without a plan, right? I pull out my phone. I can help. We can form a strategy and make a to-do list. I can check the map up there, and see what places may have more information. Law offices. Banks. The post office. "Well, we should figure out how we'll do it."

He glances over from the corner of his eye. "Right...Okay."

I look at the time. It's 11:00 a.m. now. We won't be able to do much until tomorrow. So, "Let's start by setting an alarm. 5:00 a.m.? 6? When should we wake up to get going?"

He laughs. "When my eyes open."

"I'm serious. Trust me, this works. I'll make sure we get enough sleep by setting another alarm for...I don't know...9:00 tonight? That should be good. If we follow the schedule—which is easy with reminders," I say, shaking my phone in the air to emphasize the usefulness of this great device, "then we'll be much more efficient. Otherwise—"

His smile is still there, but it looks a little forced now.

"Okay, I'll handle the alarms. Let's talk about something else." Is he taking me seriously? Moving on to the next item... "Hotels. Where are we staying tonight? Are we driving straight through or should we stop? Considering we have to stop for gas at some point, we should calculate that time in, and–"

"What the hell are you doing?"

"What? We need a plan. I'm forming a plan."

"No, you're micromanaging shit that doesn't matter." His smile's gone now, and his voice gives away his irritation.

Well, guess what buddy? This is what you got yourself into when you decided you wanted to be with me, so you'll have to get used to it. But instead of standing up for myself, I sink into my seat and look out the window. "Sorry. But it's not like we can make it up as we go. Think about it, bathroom breaks, stops for food, sleep–which we will need at some point. Those all add minutes and hours, and I don't know how long you plan on being gone, but if we're aiming to be back home by, say, Tuesday night or Wednesday morning, then we have to account for all the details."

You know what? I do know what I'm talking about. I look at my phone again. I can work this stuff out myself, and when I have a detailed itinerary, he'll see how awesome this is. I search through hotels and restaurants, selecting those that are right off the highway. I read reviews, and make a list of the best gas prices. Every now and then I see Devon look over, but I'm ignoring him. He can do the driving while I work on the navigating. We'll be a team.

About twenty minutes later, shortly after we've escaped the heavy traffic and are keeping a steady speed, Devon speaks up again.

"Let's hear it."

"What?"

"Your grand plan. I can see you're working hard over there."

I hesitate. It's like giving a presentation. I know it's good material, but will he see it that way?

"Okay..." I start. "In about an hour, there's a decent gas station with the lowest prices in the area. We'll stop there and get some snacks. And then, we'll drive straight through until dinner, where I have three places from which you can choose."

Devon swings the steering wheel to the right, throwing me off balance. I grab the door to steady myself. He pulls into the parking lot of a closed bank and slams on the brakes.

"What are you doing?" I ask.

He answers with sarcastic enthusiasm. "Never mind me. Tell me more. This is fascinating."

Oh, we're going to be a condescending bastard now? Fine. "After dinner, we'll go to a hotel where we'll get some sleep, wake up early, and get back on the road."

"Right. And listing out all this is...what? Supposed to save the day? We couldn't get through the trip without it being in writing?"

I ignore him. "*After* we get into Oregon, we'll stop for lunch. Oh yeah, breakfast will, um, either be more snacks from a gas station so it's quick, or maybe we can do the break-fast at the hotel."

He lets out his frustrated laughter as he snatches my phone from my hand. I reach for it, but he holds it out away from me like an adult teasing a child.

"I get that you have your issues, Olivia. But it doesn't give you the right to be a pain in the ass."

He shuts off my phone and fumbles with it a moment. After some careful prying, he's removed the SIM card and battery. I'm shuf-fling between feelings of anger and anxiety, and before I can think of what to say, Devon shoves the removed pieces into the glove compartment and carelessly tosses my phone into the backseat. I swing around and watch as it falls between the seat and the door, sliding out of view.

I turn back to Devon, and open my mouth to speak. Instead, he moves toward me and presses his lips to mine. His tongue steals away all my arguments until he pulls away.

"You can't–"

"Shut up and let's go."

I'm still wide-eyed, and the taste of Devon lingers on my lips as he shifts back into drive and hits the gas.

# CHAPTER EIGHT

We've made it to Santa Barbara, and Devon takes us to a small restaurant on the beach. He pulls up to valet, and a man in a black suit opens my door. It's funny. My idea of road trips includes fast food and excessive bags of chips and cookies. But it's not the case with my wealthy companion. His life of luxury continues no matter what he's doing.

This restaurant is beautiful. Outside, it's decorated with landscaped gardens and fountains that immediately put me at ease. Maybe that's why he brought me here. After ripping apart my plans–and phone–he knew this would settle me down. Relax me. Nothing with him seems unintentional, like he's always several steps ahead of the rest of the world. If he really did just pick this spot for me, I could love him for it.

Whoa. Not so fast. Let's keep that L-word under wraps.

He takes my hand and leads me through the front doors. Inside is as gorgeous with enormous windows and beach wood furnishings. The hostess spots Devon, and without him making any request, she leads us past the main floor and up a set of stairs. We find ourselves on the private rooftop where the few tables up here are partitioned off by sheer white curtains that dance in the breeze. We're seated at a table that gives us a perfect view of the ocean, and a server immediately walks over. I'm almost too speechless to order my drink.

The server leaves, and I turn to Devon. "This place is phenomenal."

"But it wasn't on your itinerary was it? Maybe we should leave..." He grins, and I playfully kick at him.

We get our drinks and order our lunch. I stick with a kale salad while Devon orders a steak and baked potato. It's blissfully quiet up here. The sounds of the waves mix with the classical music being played by a pianist in one corner.

"Is everything with you so surprising and luxurious?" I ask and add in, "And over the top, extravagant?"

"Why? Do you hate it?"

"I love it." Damn, there's that word again. But it's true. This is amazing.

We get our food and eat slowly, enjoying the moment of peace. We finish our meal and sit back, sipping at our glasses of wine. Devon's phone rings, and he excuses himself to answer it. I look out at the ocean and breathe in the crisp, salty air. Even I can admit how blissfully calm I feel. Maybe Devon can be the cure for all my ailments. I smile to myself and turn toward my Sexy Stone. He paces near a corner, intently focused on his conversation. I watch as he rubs his jawline and freezes in place. Another second later, he hangs up.

And in the peaceful quiet of this exclusive rooftop dining area, Devon yells, "Fuck yes!" interrupting everyone's meals. I look around to see a few curious faces peek over from their tables. My own cheeks go warm at the sudden attention, but Devon waltzes up to my chair and kisses me hard on the lips.

"Nothing better than being right," he says, returning to his seat. He ignores the other patrons glancing in our direction.

"Care to elaborate?"

"Yes, my theory. Which–no longer a theory, by the way. That was my P.I. He got a name."

I lean in toward him, certain things are about to get more exciting.

"M.H. Melody Hastings."

"And she is?" I mean, a name makes it easier, but that only brings up more questions.

Who is she? What does she have on Calvin Stone?

"My guy did some extra searching, including the birth records my father somehow had sealed." He drinks his wine as I tap my foot in suspense. "Melody Hastings is my mother."

Not to delve into family drama, but he didn't know his own mother's name? "I'm sorry. I need more information than that. Why didn't you learn all this before?"

"Because it was all a hunch before. I didn't want to look like a lunatic, searching for my dead mother."

"She's dead?"

"Are you not listening? My dad's paying her off, so clearly she's alive." He relaxes into his chair, and our server brings our check. He hands her a card and looks to me. "Ever since Kaidan and I were kids, we were told she was dead, that she wasn't a good person, and we were better off."

That's awful. How could you tell two little boys that about their own mother?

Devon continues, "The story goes, my dad met a stripper named Misty at Exotic Blooms, in fact–the strip club, not the florist." He winks at me, and an image of white orchids crosses my mind. "She ended up getting pregnant with twins, but soon after we were born, she was killed. Murdered. Or overdosed. Or...I don't know. Those details were always vague. But I never believed it. I always had this feeling she was still alive. But I was the only one. But now..."

Holy shit. "She's alive. You were right." This is incredible. To think, tomorrow, I can see them reunite. Devon can rebuild a part of his family he thought he'd lost forever. I'm in a hurry to get to Bandon now.

The server returns his card, and Devon signs the receipt. We sit in silence for a moment as the truth settles in for both of us, but the moment is interrupted by what sounds like an event starting downstairs outside. A beach party for the rich and famous? I look to Devon as he looks back at me with the same curious expression, so we stand up to peek over the edge of the roof. Standing at the glass wall that lines the edge, we look down to see who's making all the noise.

The paparazzi have arrived. But maybe it's not for us. *Hopefully* it's not for us. Multiple cars pull up and park, and guys with cameras hop out to join those who beat them to the restaurant. One guy, who looks laughably like a pirate in his vest, looks up and spots us. "There he is!" he shouts and points at Devon, only I hear it as "Thar 'e iz" and giggle.

Devon flinches back out of their view. "Dammit," he says. "Come on." He takes my hand as we rush across the rooftop and back through the door we entered. So much for peaceful and relaxing.

We hurry down the stairs, but at the bottom, someone recognizes Devon and calls attention to us again. All the patrons who had been happily preoccupied with their lunches are looking our way. A few pick up their phones, focusing their cameras on us. My heart pounds, and I feel like my lunch might make a reappearance. It's like an awkward scene from a movie as these, supposedly classy, people suddenly begin acting like the same vultures outside. Devon yanks me through a set of swinging doors that lead into the kitchen. Now we're behind the scenes, rushing past cooks and servers and stoves and freezers. The staff turn our way as we pass through. My cheeks warm and I duck my head down as I try to ignore the embarrassing stares from those who know we shouldn't be here. Then two large men in black suits cut us off on the other side of the kitchen. I jump and my skin turns to ice. Who are they?

I recognize one of them as Carl, the guard from Devon's condo. He says, "Mr. Stone, your car will be brought around, same place as usual. Will you be needing an escort out?"

I look from Carl to Devon. Has he been through this before?

"We'll be fine. Thanks," Devon says, and as quickly as they appeared, they seem to disappear off to somewhere else.

"Are they like the Secret Service?"

He laughs at me and pulls me to a small hallway that leads to the back door. Devon locks it, and I try to catch my breath as we stand there, waiting. "Security detail. They come in handy."

"Are they always with you? Have they been following all this time?"

"I forgot to tell you how pretty you look today."

I laugh, but really, I want to know what's up with those guys. Now seems like an odd time for compliments. Devon stands in front of me, still as calm and collected as he can be. How does one grow accustomed to these bizarre routines?

Then he kisses me. Like before, all my thoughts melt as I sink into him. He wraps his arms around me, pulling me closer, and I link my fingers into the waist of his jeans to encourage him. He tastes like white wine. He tastes like adventure.

Noise from outside the door interrupts us. The camera clowns have found us again and are snapping away through the small window.

Devon checks the time on his phone. Do they really have this choreographed down to the minute? "We're going to have to run," he says. "You ready?"

"I don't think I have a choice."

Devon's fast and smooth as he unlocks the door and shoves it open with extra force. Two of the gawkers fall flat on their asses as Devon grabs my hand and yanks me out into the sea of clicking shutters and flashing lights. We bolt down the sidewalk–Devon pushing past anyone who tries to stand in our way. My lungs burn as we sprint, but hand-in-hand with Devon, I'm certain we could fly if we wanted to. The familiar blue car turns a corner ahead of us and is coming in our direction. People are chasing behind us, and my heart is pumping wildly. The valet driver stops the car and is barely out of it, when we reach him. In one swift action, Devon hands the guy a few bills, dives into the driver's side, and pulls me in on top of him. I scoot into my seat as he yanks his door closed, shifts the car into drive and stomps on the gas pedal. Paparazzi blocking the street scatter and chase the car as we pass. There's a blur of flashes and yelling people as I settle into my seat and buckle my seatbelt.

Devon's barely broken a sweat as he navigates the streets and gets us back out toward the highway, heading north. My heartbeat steadies itself, and I find myself laughing. Giggling madly. The adrenaline coursing through me—all that excitement.

I've never felt more alive.

# CHAPTER NINE

The sun is setting as we enter a busy down-
town San Francisco.

"We're stopping for the night," Devon
says. "That alright with you?"

I've spent the last hour of this long drive
nuzzled against Devon's warm shoulder. My
stiff body begs to get out and move, so I'd be
willing to stop anywhere.

We pass bars and theaters and shops. I
peer at the clock on his dashboard. It's only
7:30, yet it feels like a different day entirely.
It's busy outside as the nightlife is taking over

the city—all the happy people dressed up and in line to be the first to get into the clubs.

Devon slows near a tall, brightly lit hotel and turns in. We follow the brick entrance to valet and get out. One attendant gets in to park while another pulls our bags from the trunk.

"I got it," Devon says and takes the bags from him. "Thanks," he adds.

He takes my hand with his free one and we go inside. A few minutes later, we're riding the elevator to the top floor. We exit, walking to the first door on our left. Devon opens it wide to reveal the massive penthouse suite awaiting. *Wow.* It's way more room than we need. Marble floors, chandeliers, and floor-to-ceiling windows overlooking the busy streets outside. This room has a tall, king size bed layered in linens and pillows in creams and deep reds. There's a Jacuzzi in one corner and a full size, private bar in another. There's a kitchen already stocked with the staples and an oversized bathroom. The center of the penthouse has white leather couches and a flat screen TV mounted to a large column that extends up through the ceiling. The room is chic and modern, but really, we're only going to be here one night. Was it worth the splurge?

Reality check. This probably isn't a splurge for Devon. This is simply your run of the mill overnight hotel stay.

Devon drops our bags onto the bed.

"What do you think?" he asks.

He knows this is all new to me. I should be overwhelmed by all this luxury he paid for a single night, but I'm more entranced by the sexy guy who's brought me here.

I erase the distance between us and reach up, weaving my fingers into his hair. He leans down and kisses me.

"Let me take you out," he says after he pulls away.

More adventures with Devon. This will be fun. Plus, I have the perfect thing to wear.

I take my entire bag into the bathroom so I can surprise Devon. Pulling out the red dress Maddie's loaned me, I almost second-guess if I can pull this off. But if I want to seek out a new life, this is a good start. Be the person I want to be, even if I have to fake it until it's true. So tonight, I'll be confident, happy Olivia in a smoking hot dress.

When I emerge from the bathroom, my hair is in waves down my back, the dress is formed tightly to my body–stopping at mid-thigh. My makeup is dark and sexy, and I feel somewhat balanced in my black heels.

Devon has his back turned to me as he fastens his black pants. He reaches over and pulls a dark gray dress shirt from his bag, turning around as he puts it on. He gets one look at me and is suddenly fumbling to button his shirt.

"Damn, girl."

I smile. I like getting a reaction out of him. I walk over smoothly and pull his hands from his shirt. I hold his eye contact as I work each button with ease, and when I reach the last one at the bottom, I hook my index fingers in his pants pockets and pull him closer to me. "I'm ready when you are."

Devon says the club he wants to take me to is right down the street, so we're taking advantage of the cool night air and walking. Occasionally, we get a stare from someone who recognizes Devon, but for the most part, we're like any other normal couple. I could get used to this.

We walk up to a club called Domain. A line starts at the door and runs down the sidewalk blocking the entrances to shops and 24-hour cafes. Everyone is dressed their best and excited with anticipation as they wait, fixing their clothes, smoothing their hair.

Devon leads me right to the door. He nods at the bouncer who shakes his hand, and then he lets us in with no hassle whatsoever. I glance back as we go inside to see a mix of curiosity and irritation as those behind the rope have nothing to do but wait. Never mind that part about us being a normal couple.

Inside, we're thrown into a dark room where it seems every inch of space is taken up by a body. I realize I've never actually been in a club, and I'm not sure I'm seeing the appeal now, but I'm determined to have fun tonight. The air itself seems to be occupied by the loud bass of the deejay's music. Bright lights rotate from the ceiling, seeming to dance to the rhythm as well, and I find myself occasionally blinded by looking in the wrong spot at the wrong time. I grip Devon's hand tighter as he leads me up a set of stairs to an upper floor.

We pass another man with a clipboard, but he doesn't even look at it as Devon catches his eye. Another quiet nod, and we're let in. This is too easy. I relax a little knowing Devon has full control here. We head to a bar off to the side where Devon orders us each a drink.

I look around the room, trying to recognize anyone famous, but I suck at this game. If only Maddie were here. She'd know most these people's names *and* stories.

A familiar looking woman walks by, stopping in her tracks when she sees Devon. "Hey!" she says, giving him a hug. "What are you doing up here?"

"Personal business," is all he says, handing me my glass.

She looks at me, "And you must be Olivia. So happy to meet you." She hugs me too as I try to pinpoint where I know her. Some movie or something. "Devon and I took acting classes together way back in the day. I've got all sorts of stories about him if you want to hear them."

I doubt I do. "Acting, eh?" I turn to Devon. "Actor? Rock star? What else?"

He smiles, and his friend gets distracted by someone else she spots. She hurries away, and Devon and I wander through the room as we drink.

"How does it feel to be a celebrity?" he asks.

I laugh, "Not hardly. And if my only fame in life is being attached to Devon Stone, then..." I take a sip of my fruity drink as he stops and stares down at me.

"What's so wrong with being attached to Devon Stone?" He closes the space between us, and where his body touches mine, I tingle. I drink faster, wishing we could be back in the room instead of here.

"Nothing wrong at all."

"That's what I thought." He puts his free arm around my waist and directs me to the left. "Check this out." He leads me toward another set of doors and holds one open, inviting me into the crisp night air. We're now on a balcony looking out at the rest of the busy street. It's crowded out here, but the open sky above makes up for it. We squeeze through couples dancing and groups of people clustered together talking and laughing, and we find ourselves at the edge of the balcony. I hold onto the cement wall as I peek over the edge. The line to Domain has grown even longer. To the left, other clubs are just as busy, and to the right, I can see our hotel. I smile knowing that a large part of the top floor belongs to us tonight.

"Not bad, right?" Devon says, speaking over the loud music.

I drink from my glass again. "This is pretty cool."

He smiles and speaks with a touch of sarcasm. "So good to have your approval."

If he thinks I can't take his teasing, he's in for a surprise. I snatch the buttoned fabric of his shirt and yank him closer to me, forcing him to lean down. Without saying a word, I plant my lips on his, softly at first. I tease his bottom lip with my tongue, tasting my own fruity drink on his delicious full lips. He sets his glass on the edge of the balcony and wraps his arms around the small of my back. The longer I kiss him, the more I feel him growing hard. Good to know I have his approval as well.

I give him a soft moan only he can hear as I pull away from his mouth. His intense gaze sparks with mischief, and I look forward to whatever happens later.

"You dance?" he asks.

"Not in a million years," I answer.

"Well, tonight you do. Come on." He grabs his glass and my hand and pulls me toward the open floor with all the other undulating bodies.

This will certainly lead to my own embarrassment. But I'm not me tonight. I'm whoever I want to be. And apparently that person dances...

"Holy shit. Stone!" someone yells nearby.

Devon whips his head toward the voice, and his face fills with recognition and excitement. "Seth! My man!"

"Dude. It's been a long time," Seth says. "What's your ass doing all the way up here?"

"I'm on a mission," he yells over the music. "With my girl." He motions his head toward me, and Seth looks over.

"Nice." He puts his hand out. "I'm Seth."

"Olivia." I shake his hand. *Devon's girl.*

Devon points at his friend. "This guy has been one of my best friends for as long as I can remember. Then he moved here, and it's like he fell off the edge of the earth."

"Hey. It's not like you're stuck in L.A. Get out of that shit hole. Move north."

I'm mostly smiling and nodding, amused seeing Devon so excited to see a childhood friend.

Someone comes up behind Seth and grabs him by the shoulders. "Let's go, mother fucker," he yells, hanging on to Seth and grinning wildly.

Seth looks at me. Then looks at Devon. "We're going inside if you want to join."

He squints his eyes suspiciously as he says this, and Devon nods. "Yeah, we'll catch you in there."

Seth and his friend snake their way inside and disappear.

"You okay going in?"

It's much nicer out here, but if Devon wants to see his friends. "That's fine," I say. I want to immerse myself in Devon's world tonight.

He looks at me an extra moment too long, like he's going to say something else. Then smiles and holds out his elbow for me to grab. We start toward the doors, but someone leaps into our path.

"Oh my god. You're Devon Stone, right?"

"Last I checked."

The girl who's stopped us is wearing a lime green mini skirt, and a black crop top that barely covers her boobs. Another girl practically knocks her over as she rushes to join her. This one's in a strapless, white dress that's so tight, nothing's left to the imagination. "Oh my god, it is him. We're such big fans!"

"Fans of what exactly?" he asks without a tone of friendliness in his voice.

"You know. Everything. We read news about you and follow everything, and like–"

"Fascinating."

"And who's she? Your girlfriend or some-thing?" They look at me and talk as though I'm not actually standing right here.

"This is Olivia."

"Wow. She's so lucky," the one in white says. The neon girl looks at me. "You *are* so lucky."

I have to wonder if they filled in the blanks, assuming I'm Devon's girlfriend, or if they're just really fond of my name.

"She knows she is," Devon says. And then he maneuvers us around the strange girls. "Nice meeting you both. We have to go."

They start to respond and tell us their names, but the music drowns them out and we're inside fast enough to lose them in the crowds. Devon walks us through the busy floor and down a dark hallway.

"Where are we going?"

"VIP," is all he says.

It almost makes me laugh, remembering what Maddie had said this morning about the same acronym. Oh man, I hope the liquor isn't turning me juvenile already.

"I thought we were already in VIP." Yep, it's still funny to say.

"This is more...exclusive."

He opens another door that leads to a slightly brighter room. At least I can see in here. The room is decked out in plush chairs and couches and tables. The walls are lined in thick curtains, and a private bar has a lone bartender pouring drinks for the few people up here. The other rooms may be packed, but there are only, maybe, two-dozen people in here. It's intimate. Nice.

Devon spots his friends in a corner on the other side of the room, and as we get near them, I almost come to a complete halt mid-step. The corner is set up with two loveseats and an armchair. On one loveseat, two women sit, relaxed with their drinks in hand. They seem perfectly in their element. Seth's loud friend is sitting on the edge of the armchair, his elbows resting on his knees, and Seth...

Seth is kneeling on the floor, leaning over a coffee table, and snorting a line of white powder.

# CHAPTER TEN

No. This is no longer "pretty cool". This is the opposite of that. I squeeze Devon's hand as though it were the international signal for, "Let's get the hell out of here!" He pulls me to the empty loveseat, and I sit close to him. Our thighs touch, and I try to convince myself that Devon has this under control, and my physical closeness to him will make me more comfortable with this situation.

Seth finishes doing...what he's doing. He stands up and grabs ahold of one of the girls, pulling her up by her hand. He spins her once as if showing her off and says, "Your turn, love."

She giggles and gets lost kissing him before she leans down and lines herself up with the next row of cocaine. I sit up straighter, sick to my stomach. I look around. No one seems to notice–or care. The bartender who's in our direct view has to be able to see what's going on, but he's doing nothing to stop it as though it's completely fine.

I turn back to see the girl rubbing at her nose. Then she swivels around to face Seth who took her place on the loveseat. She crawls closer to his lap. He leans down to kiss her, and when he sits back up, her head stays pressed against his thigh as she nestles in close to his crotch. They need a damn room. But again, no one except me seems to take notice of how inappropriate–and illegal–this is.

"Your turn D-Man," the guy in the chair says, and it takes me a second to realize he's talking to Devon.

"No thanks," he says.

"Come on," Seth insists. "Like old times."

"I'm good." Devon's voice is calm. He's hardly fazed by this and doesn't even seem uncomfortable declining their offer. The other nameless girl happily accepts Devon's turn, and I sit here, gulping my drink, trying to mask my own horror.

The faster I swallow, the less nervous and jittery I feel. But my mind still races. If we're caught by the wrong people, can't I get in trouble too? Am I some sort of accomplice right now?

I finish the last of my cocktail, and get up for another. Devon offers to get it, but I need to walk away for a second. I reach the bar, and lean into it, letting the wood top support me.

"Vodka cranberry," I tell the bartender. "Extra vodka, please."

He makes my drink and hands it over. I'm watching for any sign from his body language and facial expressions that he's about to call the cops or something. But he seems friendly and relaxed, a lot like Maddie when she's running the bar.

*This can't possibly be normal*, I want to scream.

I return with my new drink. Devon links his fingers with mine and squeezes my hand. He leans toward me and brushes his lips against my neck. A chill runs down my spine. Every touch from him feels so good. My dizzy head focuses only on him. Maybe I can shut everyone else out.

I listen as Devon and Seth update each other on their lives. Alcohol settles into me, and I'm back to that pleasant floating feeling that makes me careless that I'm surrounded by drug addicts.

Right as this drink disappears, the two girls stand up. One says, "We need the restroom. We'll be back."

The other one looks at me. "Want to come, Olivia?"

I'm not sure when they learned my name. Maybe they read it, but I do need the bathroom, so I stand up. "Yeah, why not?"

I follow their lead as we stumble to the women's restroom. After I come out of my stall, I walk to the sinks, standing next to Seth's date as she fixes her makeup.

I'm washing my hands as she says, "I'm Naomi, by the way." She smudges at her eyeliner. "And my friend is Caroline."

As if on cue, Caroline emerges from her stall and joins us. I try to smile and play nice while the alcohol I've consumed takes control. The black and white tiles in the bathroom melt into a gray tone. I take a calming breath, but the floor feels like it's sliding beneath my feet.

Naomi asks me, "Are you okay? You, like, seem so down."

"I'm fine. I'm just a little drunk, I guess. And a little tired."

She reaches into her purse. "You want a quick hit? That'll wake you up."

Did she just offer me drugs? I stop her before she can show off her stash. "No—no thank you."

"She doesn't do drugs," Caroline says, drying her hands.

Maybe I shouldn't have come in here. Are they going to judge me because I'm not into that? "No, I don't. Sorry." Right now, I don't give a damn that they do. My only desire is to not be standing anymore.

"Nah, it's cool," Caroline says. "I was only stating the obvious."

Oh, okay then. She fixes her lipstick. I look at my own reflection realizing how tired I look. Long drives have that tendency of making me look sleep deprived.

"Here." Naomi reaches into her bag again. I'm afraid of what might come out, but she only clutches concealer. I let her dab it under my eyes. "It has extra oils and stuff to wake you up, and from what I've heard about Devon, you're going to want to be awake as late as possible."

I can think of a ton of things that could mean, and I see my cheeks redden in the mirror. We leave the bathroom, but aren't ten steps out when some guy in a white dress shirt stops in front of me. He reeks of cigarette smoke, and his hair is greasy and slick, reminding me of motor oil. My head whirls, and I need the wall for support. I back into it, and the guy steps closer.

"What's your name, pretty girl?"

Who is this creep? He needs to get away from me. I want to get back to Devon. I need to sit down. I'm too drunk to remember what he just asked me.

Caroline shoves the guy to the side. "Back the hell away, asshole. She's with someone."

Naomi puts her arm around my shoulders and directs me back toward Devon. I could cry from gratitude. I must be *too* drunk and quickly approaching the stage of being over emotional. But I was horrified by these two, yet look how friendly they are. Naomi and

Caroline—I could see them being my friends. I really need to stop being an uptight jerk.

My thoughts are interrupted as we enter the room where my Devon waits. Two men wearing jeans and t-shirts push past us.

I hear one say, "He better be here. And he's fucking dead if he is."

They're large, buff, livid. And they're heading toward the back corner of the room.

Oh god. They weren't talking about Devon, were they? But then, how would they know he was here?

"Fuck. It's Wayne," Seth says, standing up.

"You. You little shit." One guy thrusts his finger at Seth. "We need to talk."

Devon lounges in the couch, hardly caring that these guys are huge and could pummel us all. He looks from the guys and back to Seth with a sigh. "What did you do this time?"

Seth smiles and mocks his aggressor. "Have I angered you in some way, Wayne?"

"You playing games now?" Wayne cracks his knuckles. "Let me make it clear for you."

Wayne and his buff friend stomp closer as he continues yelling. "You come to my house. Fuck around with my sister. Steal my stash." Now he points at the table. "That's it there, isn't it? You wasting it on these assholes too?" He looks around at the group of people and his eyes land on Devon and darken. "Fucking Stone."

Devon stands up and gets between the guys and Seth. I back up toward the bar to add distance to this drama. Naomi and Caroline walk around Wayne to get back to their guys.

Devon steps closer to Wayne. "Why don't you leave?" He's not asking. He's insisting with his authoritative tone.

"I have a funny story for you Devon Boy. The other night. There's a knock at my door. A beautiful goddess is standing at my doorstep, her little heart broken...by you."

Is he referring to Kennedy? Devon holds his ground, his face devoid of expression. "I'll say it again. You need to fucking go."

"My story isn't through. She was all sorts of sad. So I fixed her. With my cock." Wayne bursts out laughing, and his friend joins him.

One second, Devon is standing a couple feet from the guy. The next, he's in his face. "We're done here," he says. "Get out."

"Let me know when you're done with the next one. I can take good care of her too."

I cringe with revulsion, and Devon lunges at Wayne, punching him with a hell of a right hook. Just as quickly, Wayne's friend pushes Devon back, but he responds fast. The sound of Devon's fist hitting slick skin echoes through the room, and he shoves the guy down. Seth and his friend are there kicking him now while Wayne tries to get ahold of Devon. He gets one shot in, hitting Devon in the face. Devon hardly flinches, but I do. It's all happening so fast. I turn back in time to see Devon slam the back of Wayne's head into a wall, and then four bouncers come running in, separating the guys and yelling.

One of them sees Devon, and I expect him to ask what happened. Instead he says, "What the hell are you doing here? We told you if this happens again..."

"Don't worry. I was just leaving."

Devon walks out of the VIP room leaving everyone without a goodbye, including me.

I rush out behind him, follow him down the hall, through the crowd, and down the stairs. As I push through the sea of bodies downstairs, I'm fuming. What the hell happened? And why did he leave me behind like that? I catch sight of the exit, and shove my way through in a rush to escape the crowd and breathe fresh air again.

I get outside and turn down the sidewalk in time to see Devon look back toward me. Wayne got him in the lip. It's split and bleeding.

"Yeah, don't worry about me. I'll find my own way out," I yell at him.

He stops walking and turns around toward me.

"What was that?" I ask, catching up to him. My legs wobble in my heels. I want to hold onto Devon for balance, but I've hit the last straw of this ridiculous night. The drug use. The nasty guy in the hall. The fucking bar brawl. A bunch of adults who have no sense of responsibility. Of decency. I'm pissed off and don't even want to touch him.

Devon answers me, "A couple of assholes holding a grudge. Let's go." He stomps off toward our hotel, and I struggle to keep pace.

"Those guys? Your friends? They were..." I look around to see we have an audience from those lining the sidewalk. I can hear the low voices of people asking, "Is that Devon Stone?" and "Who's that girl?" We need to get to the hotel before we create a scene.

We continue on in angry silence. I'd die this second if the paparazzi showed up. Devon with his busted lip and his drunken date. The stories they could make up... Inside the hotel, we silently walk back to the elevator. It's filled with tension as we wait to get up to our floor. But I refuse to speak first. Devon is the one who needs to explain.

The doors slide open and he walks out first. I follow him back into the room. When he turns back toward me, I can see his lip is starting to swell. I shouldn't–I should just be angry and not give a damn–but I go to the kitchen and grab a towel and ice. Devon drops into one of the couches and stares out the window. The view of him is intense. Against the white leather, Devon–decked out in his dark colors and sporting the aftermath of his fight–looks like some sort of villain. Hot and enraged.

I bring him the ice but sit in a different chair, crossing my arms.

"What do you want me to say?" he asks.

"Not *that*. You think I'm an idiot? What happened back there? Who were those people? And your very best friend? The one with stolen drugs that he snorted right there in front of me? What the hell was that? You can't pretend you wouldn't have known how uncomfortable that would make me, yet you brought me in there anyway?" I'm drunk and without a filter, so I keep spouting out all my thoughts. "And then those bouncers that yelled at you? They knew you. And they knew you as a problem. Obviously, that embarrassing scene wasn't the first time for you, was it? And then you have the audacity to walk out on me, leaving me there–with those people."

He holds the ice to his lip. "And you handled it fine, didn't you? Imagine if all your problems were first-page headlines on top of everything else? How the hell else do you react when shit's constantly blowing up all around you?"

"But you create your own first-page headlines. You put yourself in the news, every time. You probably wouldn't be dealing with all this if you picked better friends."

"Yeah. And the world is full of shitty people making shitty decisions. We aren't all as perfect as you, are we?"

I lean down to take my heels off, disregarding Devon's personal jabs at me.

"But even if I can't escape the old me, at least it's not me anymore. You of all people should be able to understand that."

I open my mouth to object but close it again. He *did* decline the drugs. And the fight really wasn't his fault. He was defending Seth and me...and Kennedy. I suppose I should feel better, but is this where my standards lie now?

Devon's phone rings and he tosses the towel onto the coffee table and reaches into his pocket to retrieve it. It's late. Who could be calling? It's practically a one-sided conversation after Devon's initial "Hello". He listens for a minute, says "Thanks", and hangs up.

"We have an address."

"What?"

"Melody Hastings. Name and address. Tomorrow we can find my mom."

Too much is happening right now, I can't sort through my thoughts. That's fantastic news, but that doesn't resolve everything that happened tonight. "Great."

"It *is* great, Olivia. We're getting somewhere. Not even your obsessive compulsive planning would have made it this easy. So cheer the hell up."

# CHAPTER ELEVEN

When valet brings the car to us the next morning, I take the opportunity to retrieve my phone and reassemble it. Once it turns on, I'm relieved I still have half a battery. I smooth out the skirt of my green sundress and settle into my seat. The mindless distraction will be useful on the long car ride. I don't know what to do about Devon right now. How am I supposed to be fine with everything that happened last night? Yet, at the same time, I feel guilty–like I'm overreacting. On top of it all, today is going to be huge. Devon meeting his mom for the first time? How's he going to react? And then he'll need to tell Kaidan, and who knows how that will go? And through it all, what am I supposed to do? I want to be there for him, but it's all so far out of my control. So for now, I'll be the quiet companion at his side. A *very nervous* quiet companion.

As Devon pulls away from the hotel, my phone beeps to alert me to a new voicemail. I listen and it's the same as before, only a different voice and a different company. This one is some planning agency called Elite Affairs, and they're excited to have me join their team. I've never heard of them, yet the message made it sound like I was already hired. This is too weird.

I hang up and look at Devon. His black t-shirt hugs his body, and I'm mesmerized by the way his sleeve stretches around his bicep. I want those arms around me again. My gaze trails to his hands, and then I look up at his face. He's so gorgeous. Why does he have to be stubborn and complicated as well?

I take a deep breath. Get over last night. Pretend it never happened. It was just one more bump in our roller coaster.

"I've been getting strange phone calls," I say.

"Yeah?" He doesn't take his eyes off the road.

"Well, two of them, so far. People–event planning agencies–they want me to come work for them. They don't even know me, but it's like they aren't inquiring about an interview. They sound like I already have the position."

"Makes sense."

Or not at all. "How so?"

"You worked a Stone party. That's what happens." His voice lacks tone and interest.

"But I hardly worked. And I abandoned the job before the party was even over."

"They don't care about any of that. You have connections now that others dream of."

Is he serious? Because I know some rich people, that's all I need to get a job now? The thought of it sounds fantastic. Maybe it won't be such a burden finding steady work. As I consider how much easier it can be, I feel my shoulders relax and some of the tension fade away.

"Are you worried about today?" I ask. His shoulders are stiff, and his entire posture is rigid.

Devon speeds up to get through a yellow light before it turns red. "I'm fine."

"If you want to talk about it—"

"Can I drive? Not really in the mood for conversation."

I snap my mouth shut. He's acting cold, and I return to our argument last night. We never settled it, and now it seems to be strapped in the backseat, filling the whole car with tension.

During the first hour, I watch as this Monday morning comes to life. The streets grow busier, and we power through the traffic in silence. We make it through the morning, and finish off with coffee and bagels and more silence.

During the second hour, Devon blares industrial rock, and I stare at my phone. I'm reminded of the miserable looking old, married couples at Maddie's bar. Their focus on different things even though they're sitting right beside each other. The thought makes me sad.

During the third hour, I've grown sick of the charade already. I jam my finger on the power button of his stereo, throwing us into a deafening quiet.

"I'm sorry. Okay?" If saying it will put things back to normal between us, then fine. I'll say it.

"For what?"

I sigh. "I'm sorry for not understanding all you've gone through. I know you were into...things...in the past. And I know you stopped doing them. I can assume you weren't supported much by family and friends, so the fact you were able to clean up and be a better man...that's something that should be acknowledged and appreciated."

He subtly nods. "Anything else?"

"I'm sorry for being mad at you for your friend's actions. And for defending that same friend. I mean, fist fights aren't exactly the solution for everything, but you were doing what you felt you had to."

"He insulted you too."

"And he insulted Kennedy, but I'd rather not wonder which of us you attacked him for."

I shouldn't have said that. What a dumb thing for me to mention. Devon's glare confirms he feels the same way.

"And I'm sorry for saying that. Of course you were defending me. And not...her."

He laughs but doesn't respond.

"And you?"

"Me what?"

"I just apologized for everything I can think of. I think it's your turn."

He furrows his eyebrows. "But you admitted I didn't do anything wrong."

Forget it. I turn back toward the window. I really don't feel like fighting again.

"I apologize for not warning you about the guys and putting you in an uncomfortable situation. Let them do things their way, and you do things your way. Keeps the peace."

I look at him, and when his gaze catches mine he adds his sexy grin to his apology.

"What about the part where you stormed out and ditched me?"

"Sure. That too. Does that cover everything?" He puts one hand out for me to take and I weave my fingers through his.

I stare at our interlocking fingers. I guess things could have gone worse last night. But aside from a cut lip, everything's fine. We're fine.

By the time we reach the little suburban town of Bandon, the sun is setting, and my body is making it apparent how long the drive was. My legs are asleep and my neck is stiff. I bend my head to the side, trying to stretch out the tired muscles, but then Devon reaches over and rubs my shoulders and my neck, and I find myself warming under his touch.

"This is exactly what I expected," he says as he navigates the neighborhood streets. It's late in the afternoon. Kids are playing outside. Dogs are being walked. "I always knew I'd find her in some suburban utopia, happily living far from the spotlight."

My pulse quickens as I realize this is it. All this driving, and all the drama along the way, and we're here. I steady my breathing and look out the window. It seems like such a peaceful atmosphere. Devon follows the GPS and finally pulls to the side of the street, parking. We weren't prepared for what we find.

We've arrived at a grungy apartment complex with overgrown landscaping and a half-dozen cars parked in the lot in front of it. Devon and I get out and walk toward the building.

"The address said 'E'. I assumed that meant 'East'," Devon says.

He looks disappointed. He'd built up a specific image, and this wasn't it at all.

I take his hand, "Hey, don't judge a woman by her crappy apartment." He's now seen mine. He knows sometimes we have to get the best that's available to us.

He squeezes my fingers. "Thank you."

We find apartment E and knock. My heart is bursting through my ribs and I shift my weight from one leg to the other as we wait for a response. From inside, I hear a lock turn and a chain unlatch. I gulp, and the door opens.

Standing in front of us is definitely *not* Devon's mother. She looks about my age. Her dark hair is styled in a pixie cut, and her ears are lined with little silver hoops. As we take the sight of her in, she evaluates us as well.

Then she slams the door shut.

I look at Devon to gauge his reaction. He pounds his fist on the door. "I need to talk to you."

"You have the wrong place," she says, her voice muffled through the door.

"Not likely. And we're not leaving until we talk." He stands their clenching his fist. We wait.

Several seconds go by when she opens the door again.

"Where's Melody Hastings?" Devon spits out before she can close us off again.

The girl's face seems to pale at the sound of the name. We're definitely in the right place.

"Melody Hastings is dead. You know that, Devon." She crosses her arms over her chest.

My thoughts are a flutter. He was told she was dead. She really is dead. But he'd believed it wasn't true, and he'd gotten so close to proving it. My heart aches for him, but the girl said "Devon". She knows him. She's hiding more.

Devon's chest rises and falls like he's trying to calm himself. "Who the hell are you then?"

The girl's dark eyes narrow and she lifts her chin. "Lex–her daughter."

Lex, her daughter. Devon, her son.

Oh shit.

Devon seems to piece it together at the same time. He shakes his head. "You're telling me you're my sister–"

"Half-sister. But blood does not make a person family." Lex leans an arm against the doorframe, another gesture to block us out. "Which is why you should leave."

She starts to close the door, but Devon wedges his foot in the opening. "I'm not going anywhere until you tell me—"

"I don't have to tell you anything. You've gone twenty-eight years without knowing or caring. What difference does it make?" She pushes the door into his foot, but Devon doesn't move.

"The difference is, I just drove 800 miles to find her. And I find you instead–my sister."

He moves back a step, the truth in his own words leaving him momentarily speechless.

"I'm not your sister. Don't ever refer to me as your sister again. All the times I could've tracked you and Kaidan down in California, I didn't. Why? Because I have no use for brothers either. I don't want any part of the Stone family. There's nothing here for you. Now go."

She slams the door, and I hear the locks move back in place. Devon turns and leans into the wall for a moment before pushing off of it and storming out of the building.

Outside, Devon pulls out his phone and starts dialing a number. He paces with the phone pressed to his ear before hanging up with no answer. "Dammit."

He dials another and waits. He hangs up. "Fucking answer, you prick!"

He walks to his car, stopping at the back of it. He slams his fist into the hood.

"Devon! Stop. Talk to me." I rush to him. "We can talk about this."

He kicks at the Camaro's fender, and I squeeze between Devon and the car. I highly doubt he'll hit me too, and I don't think he'd be happy if he dented his car out of anger.

Devon stares through me at first. His thoughts are so far elsewhere, the look on his face is as if he doesn't recognize me. But then he focuses on me and meets my gaze. His hands find my hips as he lifts me onto the trunk. Stepping forward, he kisses me. He pauses for a second, taking me in, and then rushes for my lips again. His mouth crashes into mine as his hands press into my thighs and then rub their way up my back over the thin fabric of my dress.

I'm breathless when he pulls away. His powerful hands still warming my skin with their electric touch.

Devon laughs and I'm confused.

"What?" Has he lost his mind?

"My mother's fucking dead, and I have a sister." He runs his hand through his hair.

"What do we do now?" I ask.

He stares off into the distance and then looks back toward the apartments. "What do we do now..." he repeats.

"I think we should talk," I say, trying to get him to focus. "We can make a new plan."

He shrugs. "And do what? There's nothing here. I'm done."

"There has to be something you can do–something I can do. At least tell me how I can help fix this?"

He leaves me and gets into his car. I follow and buckle my seatbelt. As he pulls away from the road, he looks at me. "You can distract me."

# CHAPTER TWELVE

Devon drives south along the coast and stops at the first hotel we find. He books a room, and even the beauty of the glamorous beachside suite doesn't ease my mood. I know I should make him talk about all this. I should come up with a solution for this mess, but what could possibly fix this blindsided blow? He can't ignore it. Once you know the truth, it won't go away. Knowing Lex exists? He can't simply forget that.

Devon drops our bags on a bench and walks back toward me. I stand with my back to the closed door, worried about him.

"What are you thinking?" I ask. "I'm sorry that you didn't find what you wanted. I'm sorry the truth is so painful, but—"

He closes the space between us. No words. Only his mouth on mine. His hands grip my wrists and force my arms over my head. I twist my hands around and grab the door-frame as he kisses my neck. My head tilts to the side and I let out an involuntary moan as his tongue presses against my skin. He kisses my collarbone and the hollow of my throat. His mouth trails along the skin barely visible above the top of my dress.

His touch—his mouth—feel amazing, but it's not what we should be doing. "Talk to me Devon."

Devon buries his face in my hair and inhales.

"You smell good." His voice is gruff, and he sounds like he's about to devour me. My body seems to scream, *Oh, please do.* "Every part of you smells good. Tastes good."

My breathing quickens as I grow more excited. Okay, we'll talk later. It's like he's ignited me, and I want to give him everything he wants.

I move in close to his ear and whisper, "How would you know what I taste like everywhere?"

I barely get the last syllable out when Devon reaches down under my dress and grabs my ass pulling my hips toward him.

I'm trying to catch my breath when he growls into my ear, "Then educate me, Miss Margot."

I try to kiss him, but he brings one hand up, gripping my jaw and holding my head in place. There are mere inches between my mouth and his, but all I can do is stare into his icy glare. He holds his gaze on my own as his other hand follows along the elastic of my panties, tracing a line with his finger that sends shockwaves through me.

His hand plunges beneath the thin fabric, and his fingertips against my sensitive, aching skin make me want to cry out from the anticipation. I feel like he's taken over every sense. I close my eyes and my mind fills with Lust List Devon. Shirtless, hot, wet Devon. I savor his intoxicating scent—his cologne mixed with the musky natural smell of sweat. I open my eyes, and here's the real Devon, angry disappointed Devon. His adrenaline and rage seems to linger on his skin, and my breathing grows more unsteady as I watch him watch me.

I want him to take me. I want him to do whatever he wants.

I know I'm wet, and when his hand presses hard against my aching folds, he lets out a low moan. Now he knows it too. He moves his hand around in a slow circle, and fire shoots up into my core. His touch doesn't lighten as he slides up, stopping when his fingertips reach my clit. With one finger, he moves in a slow line, up and down, and my hips involuntarily lift, inviting him to do more.

He still holds my head firmly in place, and his eyes seem to scan my face observing my reactions—how my eyes can hardly focus on him. How each time he moves his fingers, I give a soft moan.

Then he leans in and his lips crush into mine. I can barely breathe as he kisses me with force. His fingers find my wet opening, and he pushes one inside me.

I let out a stifled moan that travels from my lips to his.

He pulls his finger out and then penetrates me again. This time two fingers. He curves them up and finds the one spot that makes me lose control. He's coaxing me with those fingers, and I try to keep quiet.

Devon pulls his mouth away from mine, and I find myself staring up into the pitch-black pupils of his intense eyes.

My chest rises and falls in deep, staggered breaths. Heat floods me from inside, and I feel my muscles growing tighter and tighter. My knees shake, and I don't know how I can hold myself up anymore.

He bites my earlobe and whispers, "Come for me."

His hand thrusts, and I can only wish it weren't his hand at all. I close my eyes imagining, if this feels as good as it does, what would it be like to have him on me? In me? Our pleasure building up at the same time?

In and out, his movements are smooth, and I quickly feel myself coming unbound.

I shove my face into the side of his neck to muffle the noises that escape me as my muscles contract around his fingers and I come. Intense waves rush through me, and Devon's hands don't abandon me until I've settled and come back to planet Earth. I'm gasping for breath when he pulls away.

He gives me his sexy grin as the same fingers that just brought me pleasure enter his mouth. He slowly pulls them out, holding my eye contact the whole time. I feel my cheeks flush. I can't tell if I'm mortified or ready for round two.

"Yeah," he says, "you definitely taste good."

I rush to his mouth, kissing him, begging him for more. His hands run down my back and find my ass. He squeezes and pulls me even closer. The thin fabric covering me isn't forgiving as his jeans rub against me, making me squirm—my body too sensitive from that orgasm. And his hard-on is all too apparent beyond the rough texture of his jeans.

Devon pushes me toward the bed. I move quickly, eager to get him on me, but he catches up behind me, and I stop in my tracks as I feel his breath on my neck. Chills rush through me, and I spin around to face him. As I do, he takes another step closer. With no room between us, every step he takes forces me backward, and one step too far, the bed hits the back of my legs. I start to lose my balance, but Devon catches me with one arm. In one swift move, he pulls my dress over my head. Only in my bra and panties, I feel cold, but he brings me up against him again, and I'm instantly on fire. My hands get to work fidgeting with his belt. I don't know how he plans for things to go, but I do not want Devon Stone dressed anymore.

I yank the belt from his jeans, tossing it on the floor. I reach under his t-shirt and graze my nails along his skin tracing the bottom indent of his abs. When I reach his sides, I bunch up the shirt in my hands and push it up, urging him to take the damn thing off. Now I have him shirtless, his hair disheveled, his eyes on me.

I unbutton his jeans, but before I can unzip them, he pushes me backward, making me fall onto the bed. I can't help but laugh at how amazing I feel—my natural high of being near Devon. I kick off my sandals as he finishes undressing. I'd say he takes my breath away but it's not that at all. In fact my breathing intensifies, my senses come to life. I sit up and reach for him, longing for him to touch me, but he takes a step back, leaving me on the bed, wanting. Waiting.

He walks to his bag, rummaging through for a second and pulls out a condom. We both came prepared. We both anticipated this. He comes back to me, and I feel like I'm on display as he evaluates me, taking in my messy hair, my heaving breasts, my barely-covered body. My legs tremble as they dangle off the side of the bed. Without a word, he unlatches my bra and yanks down my panties, tossing both to the side.

Devon hovers over me and kisses my forehead, my cheek, my lips. Gorgeous, naked Devon kisses my bare shoulder and then stands up straighter and grabs my knees, pulling my legs up and urging them to wrap around his body.

I try to imagine what I must look like to Devon—my hair cascading in untamed waves over my shoulders, my naked body clinging to his naked body. I smile hoping he likes what he sees.

He gives me a sexy half-grin. "You're beautiful," he says, and I feel my cheeks flush as I smile back at him. He runs his hands up my thighs, grabs my hips, and thrusts me toward him. Now I can feel his hard length pressed against my skin.

I move myself against him, and he leans down, his eyes intent on me, his grin long gone. He tangles his hand into my mess of hair as if wrapping boxing tape around his fist. I feel his hand against my head, and he tugs my hair, the sensation bordering the threshold of pleasure and pain. He's pulled my head back, exposing my neck, and my breath catches.

"Stay still," he growls.

But I can't. I want him like he wants me, and him taking his time, teasing...it's too much to bear. I take a deep breath as ecstasy rolls through me. Devon's mouth finds my neck. He kisses and sucks and nibbles. I part my lips but stay silent.

"Don't move," he says.

I stay frozen in anticipation as he leans up. The second his hands are off me, I crave his touch. My heart pounds. I hear the sound of a foil wrapper ripping. I take a deep breath and close my eyes pleading for him to get in me. And then he touches me again. His erection teases my opening, and I wrap my legs around his waist again. I smile as he leans down over me again.

"Look at me." His demands turn me on, and I obey.

His eyes are dark with lust, so I tease him again, rubbing myself against him and arching my back.

I try to speak. "I think I'll always make you angry right before—"

My words are cut off by my own cry of pleasure as Devon enters me in one swift motion. He fills me deep, and I forget what I was saying. My hands clutch the bed's quilt. In a smooth rhythm of in and out, Devon explores me from inside. His hand trails along my face, my jaw, my breasts. He puts more weight on me, as he drops down closer. The room spins, and my temperature rises, as he rests one arm next to my ear and reaches his other arm underneath the small of my back, lifting my hips higher. He pulls back and rams me with more force. A loud "oh" escapes me. I turn my head toward his arm, pressing my mouth into his hot, tanned skin. I savor his salty taste as he thrusts even harder. My body on fire, my muscles weakening, I give all of myself to Devon. He holds me up, supports my body, claims me. The tension in me builds as he persists, his own grunting encouraging me to let go. Again.

I swallow hard as the first shudder runs through me. My tingling fingers grip the flesh of his back. My nails dig in, and he pushes into me faster. Stars flash through my vision as the room goes out of focus. The entire world consists of me and Devon. It's just us. It's... it's... Like a wound rubber band being pulled tighter and tighter, my entire body breaks loose. I scream out as I come again,

ecstasy overtaking me, and I feel myself con-
tracting around his length. More moans escape from me as I feel him reach his own
release. His breathing is staggered and angry
as he comes inside me, and when the world
seems to settle again, we both collapse in a
heap onto the mattress. Devon rolls to one
side, and I turn to face him. Wrapping one leg
over his, I try to minimize the space between
us. He pushes my hair away from my face, and
I lean close to kiss him, appreciating the
sheen of sweat on his skin.

His eyes, still dark with lust, stare at me as
his breathing settles. He wraps his arms
around me, and I watch as he relaxes. He
didn't want to talk. He wanted a distraction.

And I gave it to him.

# CHAPTER THIRTEEN

Somewhere in the night, we found our way beneath the sheets. I could've stayed there for days with Devon, but as the sunlight snuck its way into my dreams, waking me up, I found myself alone in bed with a Devon-sized indent in the mattress next to me. I still reach out as though I'll touch him, but my hand only finds cool linen. As the new day settles into me, the rest of my surroundings come into focus.

Bright streams of sunshine embrace the room, and I can hear the shower running in the bathroom. We do have a long trip back. Guess it's time to get started.

I climb out of bed, wrapping a tangled sheet around me, and subtle aches remind me of last night. I smile as I look around for my bag. Right next to Devon's where he left it on an upholstered bench. The symbolism might be cheesy, but looking at those bags side-by-side, it feels like so much more. Two bags, two people, two hearts. Okay, I'm making myself gag now, but I can't deny this is starting to feel like a relationship. But I'll keep that to myself for now.

I dig through and find clothes for the day. Stepping into my jeans, I take notice of Devon's bag lying open. T-shirts and denim poke out from him sorting through and grabbing what he needed. And an envelope peeks out from one side. I recognize it as the same white envelope he stole from his father's study. The will.

Yesterday was awful. With our expectations so high, the fall to reality was that much harder, especially for Devon who thought, for certain, he'd get to see his mother again. A lump forms in my throat as I consider all the lies in the Stone family. What would he do now? How could I help?

I pull out the will. Maybe there's more information in here that can help us think of what to do next. *Us.* That sounds so good to me now. Of course we can get through this mom ordeal. But as I free the envelope from Devon's duffel bag, something else inside rattles, falling deeper to the bottom. I could almost ignore it, but it sounded like...

I look over the edge, feeling horrible now that I'm officially snooping. But there, in the corner at the bottom, I see a little tin case. A metallic blue and small enough to fit in a pocket. But there's no questioning the noise I heard from inside it. My nerves race as I return the will and pull the box from his bag. *Please, no, Devon. Please.* I listen intently at the sound of the running water. If this is what I think it is, then what do I do?

I lift the lid.

A small, plastic bottle. And a little bag. If only it were that harmless.

The little amber bottle is filled with pills. White ones, yellow ones. Blue. The white label on it reads *Lucas Shelton.* But it's not even those that crush my heart. I rub my stomach, trying to hold in the raging feelings brewing deep in me. My eyes well with tears as I lift the bag. Pinching it in between my thumb and index finger as if any more contact will burn my skin, I hold it up. Tiny dents and creases in the well-worn plastic seem to act like arrows, pointing at the white powder inside.

He said it was all in his past. I *saw* him turn down drugs right in front of me. Was it all an act? He packed for a short trip, and this is what he brought. I drop the bag back into the tin box and shut the lid.

He lied. He's been lying.

I squeeze my eyes closed and open them again. What am I supposed to do? I sit against the bed staring at the box until I hear the water shut off. He's going to know I went through his stuff. How do I explain? No, I'm not the bad guy here. He doesn't want me assuming things about him. He told me himself to ask him straightforward when I needed to know something, and right now...I fucking needed to know.

I place the tin box on the nightstand next to me and cross my arms, watching the bathroom door.

When Devon emerges, I almost don't have it in me to confront him but it's too late. He towel dries his messy hair as he walks out of the bathroom, wearing a pair of cargo shorts, no shirt. He looks delicious, but his eyes land on me. I'm trembling, and the tears won't stop. He raises his eyebrows, catching on that something is wrong.

I look to the end table, and Devon's gaze follows. I watch him as he studies the blue box before looking back at me. He doesn't say a word—and instead lets out an audible sigh.

My voice shudders as I speak. "I won't make a single assumption. You tell me what this is."

"It's nothing," he says as he strolls to his bag and pulls out a shirt, yanking it over his head and stretching it over his body. "Stay out of my stuff."

Images of sleeping with him last night run through my mind, but now they hurt. There's a throbbing in my chest and not enough oxygen in this room.

"It's not nothing, Devon." I stand up and try to keep my voice quiet. "You told me the pills were left at your place. You told me you weren't doing anything like this anymore."

"I also told you to lighten up. Relax and mind your own business."

He's packing his bag, and I'm furious, ready to completely lose it. "Are you kidding? You lied to me. Everything you said about your history being a thing of the past, about not doing drugs anymore, about these exact pills specifically. You told me to trust you. To give you more credit. I did. And you lied. What else have you been keeping from me?"

He doesn't answer and instead returns to the bathroom, throwing his wet towel on the tile floor. I follow behind him. He's not getting away with this one so easily.

"I want answers, Devon. I'm not leaving with you until I get them."

"What answers do you need? Better yet, what answers do you *want?*"

My chest grows heavier as I wipe a tear from my cheek. "I want the truth. I want you to answer–"

"Wasn't yesterday an answer enough? My mom's dead. I have a surprise sister who hates me. You see what I deal with–the random shit that I have to take? Like hell am I going to go through all this shit without...help."

He doesn't care at all that he lied to me. "You consider those help? What do they do? Make you high? Make you pass out–"

"They detach me from this hellhole called life. Separate me from the harsh reality that I was born into something I didn't want."

Great. And while he's numb to the real world, where does that put me? I don't know which hurts more—the fact he lied or that I still don't know anything about the real Devon.

"What?" he asks, standing in front of me, an annoyed expression on his face. The same expression he got when he took my phone apart—when I was the one going overboard.

But that's not what this is. I'm not overreacting. A flutter in my stomach makes me second guess that. Maybe there's more to it. Maybe his reasoning is genuine. Maybe I can handle it.

No. I can take risks with Devon. I *want* to take risks with him. But I won't compromise on this.

I look up at him, tears stinging my eyes. I'm a fool. Standing here, shaking, as if I'm completely helpless. But if Devon wants to take charge of his own life this way, then I can do the same.

I walk through the room, picking up my dress, my bra, my panties–the clothing tossed aside in last night's lust. I force back my urge to scream as I step into my sandals and thrust the dirty clothes into Maddie's duffel bag. That's how I feel now too. Dirty. Giving in to my lust with a man I, apparently, can't even trust.

"What the hell are you doing?" he asks, walking over to me.

"Have you been taking pills the entire time since we met?" I sling the duffel bag over my shoulder and pick up my purse.

"You aren't going to tell me what I can and can't do."

"No. But I can tell you what *I* can and can't do, and I can't be with you if you're going to– if that's," I nod toward the tin box, "the lifestyle you choose."

Devon tries to grab my hands, but I flinch and move toward the door.

"Okay Miss High and Mighty. Educate me about my lifestyle since you seem to know so much."

I stand there in silence. I want to run away, but where the hell will I go. Hundreds of miles away from home, and the only person I have to rely on has been lying to my face.

*I can rely on myself.*

Devon turns his back on me, instead walking to the oversized windows and staring out at the ocean. "That's right. You *don't* know. And maybe you shouldn't know. It's obvious you can't handle it–that you're so stuck up in your ways, you can't let anyone else live their life how–"

"Devon, do you even hear yourself?!" I'm losing it. My entire body is shaking now. Tears stream down my face. I choke back a sob. "You've been self-medicating to detach yourself from everything. How is that any way to live? How am I supposed to ever know you when you keep yourself from the entire world? From me?"

He turns back in my direction. The back-drop of the serene Pacific is an uncomfortable contrast to the tension in Devon's body and the look of utter frustration and contempt on his face. "I don't like my life, Olivia. And nei-ther would you. Trust me when I say–"

"I can't." I open the door, not having any clue what I'll do if I leave–*when* I leave. My trembling hand grips the doorknob tightly as if I can transfer all my anger to it. I steady my voice. "I can't trust you. That's the problem. And I don't think I can be with someone who can't face his own life–his own problems."

"You mean like you? Tell me Olivia. How long have you been running from *your* life? If our pasts are following us wherever we hide, then what's your excuse? You aren't exactly facing your problems, so don't be a damn hypocrite."

I let out an exasperated sigh. He can't turn this around on me, making me the problem. Doesn't he get that there's something be-tween us–something that can replace both our needs to escape? "I really want to be with you, but I can't be with this version of you. I don't know–"

"Don't know what? Look at you, with one foot out the door. You've already made your decision. So run away. Again."

He walks to the table, retrieving the blue box as if he's choosing sides. I look from him to the bed behind him. Did last night really happen? I divert my eyes back to Devon, taking a long look at him as if I can find the answers that way. But my gaze travels back down his arm, to his hand...to his stash of drugs.

"You think I'm the only one running away? You do it your way." I inhale a deep, shaky breath as I prepare for my next move. "And I'll do it mine."

I walk out of the room, closing the door behind me.

I can't breathe. I gasp for a single, reliable breath as I hurry down the hall and back downstairs. I can't get outside fast enough, but as soon as I get to the main doors and out on the sidewalk, I freeze and kneel down, sucking in the fresh air. What do I do now? Devon's right. I have nowhere to go. But I can't stay here. I can't let him do whatever he wants no matter how it affects me. I vaguely recall seeing a bus station on our way here, so I turn in that direction and start walking down the road, adding distance between me and a man I was certain meant more to me than a sexy tryst between the sheets.

Once I feel I can breathe again, I pull out my phone and confirm the bus station several blocks away. I can do this. I'll buy a one-way ticket back home and can be in L.A.–in my own bed–late tonight or early tomorrow. Then life can go back to normal.

But what's normal now?

I can't simply let Devon go. When I'm with him, I come to life. He can't tell me he doesn't feel the same. All the times he's gone out of his way for me, I know there's more to us. But it's his turn to call the shots. I know what I

want. It's up to him to decide what he wants—
*who* he wants.

My mind races as I quicken my pace, getting closer to my destination. Devon's words
flash through my thoughts.

*"How long have you been running from
your own life?"*

This time, I'm not running away. I left, yes.
But this time I'm running toward something.
I'm running toward my future, taking control. I can make it on my own. And when I
prove that to myself, when I become a better
version of me, then maybe Devon will do the
same.

I'm running toward the possibility of a better life. Fleeing toward the chance of a great
love. As long as Devon comes to see it too.

I reach the bus station and buy my ticket
from an old man with white hair and round
glasses. I glance toward his left hand to see
he's married. I bet he had to take chances for
his great love as well. And I bet it paid off in
decades of happiness.

I smile at him as I pay and then clutch my ticket in my hand as I take a seat on a bench to wait. A thousand thoughts cross my mind, mostly wanting to change my mind and hurry back to Devon and that luxurious hotel suite. But I push all thoughts aside and focus. I have no excuse. I'm going to prove it to Devon. And to myself. I can face the nightmares of my past. I can take care of myself.

The bus arrives and I settle into a seat, leaning my head against the headrest and closing my eyes, breathing through my own nerves.

I gaze down at my phone. What was Devon doing right now? Did he leave yet? Or did he stay behind to...I don't want to think about it. I'm confident it's not the end for us, not yet. I just need him to realize he's so much more than his family name–than his reputation.

A tap on my shoulder interrupts my thoughts. I turn to see a girl a year or two older than me holding her laptop in her lap and gawking. "Are you Olivia Margot?"

"Yes," I answer. "Why?"

She turns her laptop to show me what she'd been looking at. *ScandalLust*. I almost roll my eyes. A photo of Devon and I made the front page with the headline: *Has Devon Stone met his match?* Maybe *ScandalLust* can answer that for the both of us.

"Are you really his girlfriend?"

No? Yes? I'm not sure where we stand. All I can do is smile at the girl.

She grins from ear to ear as she goes back to reading about me and Devon online. "You are so lucky," she says, her eyes never leaving the screen.

I settle back into my seat, wanting her to forget I'm here.

*You are so lucky.*

God, I hope so.

THE LUST LIST: DEVON STONE

# THIRD DEGREE

MIRA BAILEE

Available Now

# THE LUST LIST

*The Lust List - Take Your Pick*
They're the world's sexiest bachelors. The men of *ScandalLust* mag's infamous Lust List are young, wealthy, and, oh, did we mention? *Hot*.

When scandal follows them everywhere, there's no hiding from the cameras. They're irresistible, insatiable—and talented in all the right ways. Every woman wants them. But these playboys won't be easy to catch...

# THE LUST LIST DEVON STONE

*by MIRA BAILEE*

*FIRST TASTE*
*SECOND CHANCES*
*THIRD DEGREE*
*FOUR LETTERS*

# Acknowledgments

I'm humbled by the support and encouragement I've received. The second book in Devon's series wouldn't have been possible without the enthusiasm and expertise of so many wonderful people.

Nova Raines, thank you for creating this world alongside me.

I'm forever grateful for Jamie Rich, my fearless beta; Nicole Bailey at Proof Before You Publish–the personification of a big white-out pen; and Marina and Jason of Polgarus Studio who turn my manuscripts into perfect ebooks.

And to my family and friends, and of course, my readers, you all make my job the greatest job of all.

Thank you.

# About Mira Bailee

Mira Bailee, a beer-brewing librarian, has been writing leisurely, scholarly, and professionally for the past twenty years.

While she's always maintained a high standard of chaos in her daily routine, *The Lust List* allows her to pass on some of her hectic lifestyle to her characters. Her storytelling balances humor and pleasure with sincerity and conflict, providing a wild ride of human emotions.

In the past she studied filmmaking and screenwriting and determined what goes on behind the scenes is just as tantalizing as what's seen in front of the camera. This revelation is the basis for her inspiration for *The Lust List*.

www.ingramcontent.com/pod-product-compliance
Lightning Source LLC
Chambersburg PA
CBHW021459250626
47154CB00004BA/1435